MURDER AT THE JAZZ CLUB

THE KITTY WORTHINGTON MYSTERIES, BOOK 7

MAGDA ALEXANDER

Heart Nine Publishing

ISBN-13: 978-1-943321-23-0 (EBook)

ISBN-13: 978-1-943321-26-1 (Paperback)

Hearts Afire Publishing

CHAPTER 1

WORTHINGTON HOUSE, MAYFAIR, LONDON

SATURDAY 3 MAY 1924

*E*AGER FOR BREAKFAST, I breezed into the dining room at Worthington House thankful that, today being Saturday, there'd be no need to rush through the meal. The Ladies of Distinction Detective Agency would be closed.

As I wished everyone present a good morning, I noticed one person missing. "Where's Mother?"

"She'll soon be here, Kitty," Father answered. "She's not feeling quite the thing."

That was concerning news. "Is she ill?"

"No. Only worn down. She's taken on much too much the last several months."

Ladies Lily's and Melissande's complexions took on identical rosy hues, more than likely from guilt. Since March, Mother had been shepherding both young ladies through

1

their debut season. That had meant not only numerous visits to the modiste to arrange for new frocks, but attending numerous balls, theatre outings, and whatever other events social hostesses devised.

Lady Emma's expression communicated a similar unease. My partner in the Ladies of Distinction Detective Agency had moved to Worthington House when a previous investigation had turned deadly. Although she did not participate in the social season like the younger ladies did, Mother tended to fret about her station in life.

Nor was I blameless. My involvement in the detective agency was a worry to Mother. It had eased somewhat when I'd become engaged to Detective Chief Inspector Robert Crawford Sinclair, and even more when I'd settled on our wedding date. Still, she wasn't comfortable with my lady detective activities, and she wasn't even aware of the more dangerous ones.

I would have asked more questions about Mother's state of health, but just then she walked into the room, perfectly coifed and dressed. But there was an air of fragility about her I didn't like.

"Good morning. I apologize for my tardiness," she said.

Once everyone returned her greeting, I sought to reassure her. "We don't keep to a schedule on Saturdays, Mother. You're allowed a bit of a lie in."

"Yes, of course," she replied.

After she filled her plate and took a seat next to Father, I brought up the subject that was uppermost in my mind, and I daresay, the others as well. "Father was just saying you were a bit worn out."

"Afraid so, dear. With dear Ladies Lily and Melissande's debut season"—she tossed them a sweet smile—"your wedding to arrange, the Ladies Benevolent Society gala, and Margaret's fundraiser, my time is not my own. It seems I've reached the point where I can no longer cope. Doctor Crawley suggested a period of rest each day."

My concern rose to a new level. "You visited Doctor Crawley?" Mother never did that. Whenever she felt ill, her maid, Cummings, tended to her. She had to have reached her limit to consult our family physician.

"I did. He recommended an hour or two of daily repose." She sighed. "How I'm going to get everything done is beyond me."

"Mildred," Father said. "You need to relinquish some of your responsibilities. Surely, someone else can take on the Ladies Benevolent Society Gala."

"Who?" Mother asked. "No one is as qualified as I am."

"There must be someone." Father gently covered one of her hands with his own. "You can't continue this way, my love."

Father had to be seriously worried if he addressed Mother with that endearment. Being of a private nature, he almost never did that in public. Something needed to be done.

"May I make a suggestion, Mother?" I asked.

"Of course, dear."

"There are four young ladies in this room who are more than capable. We can take some of those responsibilities off your hands. If we run into any impediments, we can discuss them with you. You can be the general, and we can be your troops. Can't we ladies?" I pointedly gazed at the ladies in question.

A chorus of "Absolutely," "Of course," and "We would love to help" issued from all of them.

"There you are, Mildred," Father said. "How does that suit you?"

"I suppose it could work." But Mother didn't appear entirely convinced.

"Splendid," I said. "After breakfast, we'll convene in your parlor and assign tasks. Right, ladies?"

Another round of choruses followed.

It was a jolly group that met in Mother's parlor once we were done with our meal. In no time at all, Ladies Lily and Melissande offered to help Margaret with her women's causes in general, and her fundraiser specifically. They would telephone Margaret to inform her of the change as soon as the meeting ended. Lady Emma volunteered to take over the gala. It made total sense since she was the one most familiar with the members of the Ladies Benevolent Society. I, of course, would handle those responsibilities connected with my wedding day.

Once all questions were answered, Mother dispatched Ladies Lily and Melissande so they could telephone Margaret and suggested Lady Emma head to the library so she could acquaint herself with the voluminous gala files Mother had handed to her.

That left Mother and me to discuss—heaven help me— my wedding day.

Without wasting time, she retrieved a thick folder from a desk drawer. To my horror, the thing was several inches thick.

"Is it as much as all that?"

"Oh, this is only one folder. There are several more."

I gulped.

This one, labeled *Kitty's Trousseau*, contained not only a list of dresses, undergarments, and so forth, but several sketches of said items. "As you know, your wedding gown and trousseau are well in hand. Angelique is a treasure. She'll make sure you're properly attired on your wedding day and have a proper wardrobe that reflects your newly married status."

"Yes, indeed, Mother." I'd already visited the modiste

4

several times to discuss my wedding gown and begin the fitting process. As for the rest of my trousseau, it would not prove a hardship. I adored fashion. Of course, what I thought was appropriate for a married woman differed greatly from my mother's. Her choice of wedding night wear consisted of a cotton gown that covered every inch of me from my neck down to my toes. Needless to say, it was not what I had in mind. With Angelique's assistance, I'd designed a splendid peignoir set that was, let's just say, quite a bit more revealing.

"Now, dear, about the church." Mother retrieved another appropriately marked folder. "St. George's on Hanover Square has been reserved so that's one task you won't need to worry about. Although as the wedding day grows closer, we'll need to concern ourselves with other matters, such as the flowers and such."

Another folder was retrieved. This one was titled *Wedding Breakfast*. "The celebration will be held here, of course. We'll have a guest list of 300, as that's all we can comfortably fit into our ballroom. You won't need to concern yourself with the tables, chairs, and so on. But one thing you and Robert need to decide upon is the menu. You'll need to discuss that subject with him. There will be a head table where you and he will sit along with your attendants—your sister Margaret and Lady Emma and his groomsmen. He'll need to tell you who they will be. I imagine Lord Hollingsworth will be one. We'll need a second one."

"Maybe Sebastian or Ned."

"Both fine choices. He'll need to choose between them."

"Yes, of course."

She fetched another folder from which she retrieved a list. "You'll need to settle on several more items. Your wedding invitation for one. I've included a draft of the language. But, of course, you can change it to whatever you wish. I suggest we contact the wedding stationers earlier rather than later. Smythson of Bond Street is a fine one. They hold a royal warrant."

"Yes."

"Now we come to your wedding china, your crystal, your flatware, and your new furniture."

"Robert has dishes, Mother."

"They're bachelor china, dear, not married gentleman china. There is a difference. Not only that, he's now Lord Rutledge's heir. Your china, crystal, and flatware will need to reflect his newly married status as well as his position as the heir presumptive. I made a list of the best establishments to consult." She handed me a list—six each for the china, the crystal, and the flatware. "You'll need to discover Robert's preferences before you visit these establishments."

"Shouldn't he accompany me?"

"No gentleman as busy as Robert will want to visit vendors."

"I'm busy as well, Mother." The Ladies of Distinction Detective Agency had more business than we could handle. From Monday to Friday, we ran ourselves ragged.

"Yes, dear, but you're not Scotland Yard. Robert is. You have a choice as to what clients you take on. He doesn't. And then there's this to consider. Now that he's Lord Rutledge's heir"—she adored saying that and regularly mentioned it half a dozen times a day—"he will be looked upon more favorably for a promotion. He'll need to entertain not only his superiors at Scotland Yard, but your friends and family as well. I would suggest twice a month suppers when the season is upon us; less often when it's not. Which reminds me, how is Robert's cook?"

"I haven't the foggiest."

"Well, you'll need to find out. I suggest you make an appointment with Robert. The sooner the better. Tomorrow after church will be a good time to discuss what you plan to do. Now as far as ideas for patterns, I suggest you take swans into consideration."

I blinked. "Swans?"

"Yes, a swan is front and center in the Rutledge family crest. I understand one saved the life of one of Robert's ancestors."

"How did it manage that?"

"I don't know, dear. You'll need to find out."

She retrieved another folder. This one was the thickest of all. It was entitled *Furniture*. Well, no wonder. Mother loved to redecorate. There wasn't a London furniture warehouse she wasn't intimately acquainted with.

"You'll want to choose new furniture for your bedchamber. I'm sure Robert has serviceable furnishings, but you'll want to choose your own."

"But wouldn't I be sharing his room? I mean our room?"

"Yes, dear. But you'll want your own private quarters for bathing and dressing. And, of course, for those days of the month in which you're indisposed."

"But I'm rarely ill."

"Not ill, dear, indisposed." She pointedly gazed at me. "It happens every month."

Light finally glimmered. "Oh, yes, of course. I didn't know married couples slept apart during that . . . time."

"Some do, some don't. You'll want your own private space, Kitty. If for no other reason than sometimes life gets to be a bit much. Discuss it with Robert, but let it be your decision."

"Yes, of course."

Weighed down with all the folders she'd given me, I slowly made my way up the stairs to my room where I made a neat pile of them on my desk. And then I headed toward Father's study to call Robert. If I had to suffer through this lunacy, so did he.

CHAPTER 2

A TÊTE-À-TÊTE WITH ROBERT

THE FOLLOWING MORNING AFTER CHURCH, I headed to Robert's Eaton Square address with my maid Grace in tow. Robert and I might be engaged, but the proprieties still had to be observed.

His butler, Mister Grant, greeted us at the door. The older gentleman, dressed in immaculate livery, had exquisite manners as only someone who'd been trained in the very best of butlering schools possessed.

"Miss Worthington, a pleasure to see you again."

"Likewise, Mister Grant. May I introduce Grace Flanagan, my lady's maid."

"Miss Flanagan." He nodded.

"Would you be kind enough to take charge of her while I converse with Lord Robert?" In private, I referred to my fiancé as Robert. But given he was the recently acknowledged second son of a marquis, he was to be addressed with the lord tacked on to his given name. A naming custom his staff would most certainly observe as proper etiquette required it.

"It will be my pleasure. Cook and the rest of the staff are eager to meet Miss Flanagan. We've gathered in the kitchen to enjoy a repast."

"Splendid." I gazed around the space. "Where is Lord Robert?"

"Lord Robert offers his apologies. A telephone call has delayed him. He's asked me to show you to the library."

"How lovely." I'd been introduced to that room during a previous visit. It'd been October then so a cozy fire had been lit. As it was now summer, I could not expect the same. But I would surely enjoy the comforting nature of a room lined with bookshelves. "Thank you."

After Mister Grant led the way to that room, tea was soon served. I barely had time to take a sip before Robert made his appearance. As always he was immaculately dressed, this time in a three-piece grey pinstriped suit, white button down shirt, grey tie, and silver stickpin. His dark hair was carefully arranged with not a lock out of place.

"My apologies," he said. "A matter came up at Scotland Yard they wished to discuss with me."

My breath hitched. "You don't have to leave, do you?" That was often the case when Scotland Yard telephoned.

"No. They had a few questions they wished to ask. That's all."

"Good. Thank you for making time to see me."

"My darling." He kissed my cheek and sat next to me on the small brown leather sofa I'd oh-so-carefully chosen. "I will always do so."

I scrunched my face. "You won't after you hear everything we need to discuss."

"Oh?"

"We need to decide on china, crystal, and flatware

9

patterns. Before you say you have all those things, Mother assures me they're not sufficient. Not for Lord Robert Sinclair, heir presumptive to the Marquis of Rutledge." I sighed. "I brought my sketchbook so we can jot down a few ideas."

"Thank you for including me in your process. You didn't have to, though. I'll like whatever you choose."

"It'd serve you right if you find yourself staring at a great big swan in the center of a dinner plate."

He raised a questioning brow. "A swan?"

"Mother said your family crest features a swan. Apparently, one saved the life of one of your ancestors."

His shoulders shook with laughter. "Yes, you might say it did."

Confused, I asked, "What's so amusing?"

Still smiling, he said, "Do you know what *droit du seigneur* means?"

My face heated up. "Yes." Its literal meaning was 'right of a lord,' a horrible custom in which a medieval feudal lord claimed the right to have intimate relations with a vassal's bride on her wedding night.

"One of my ancestors was fond of demanding it. That changed one day when a vassal whose bride was to be, er, deflowered strongly objected to the custom. When my ancestor tried to claim his right, the vassal chased him with an axe. Legend has it he very much intended to cut off a certain part of the lord's anatomy."

"Oh, my!"

"The lord literally ran for his life—bare bottomed if the story is to be believed—toward Castle Rutledge."

I giggled. "That must have been quite a sight."

"Indeed. The vassal, who was young and fleet of foot, was within reach of the lord when fate intervened. You see, they had to skirt a lake where a bevy of swans had settled down for the night. Furious to have their slumber disturbed, they emerged, squawking and flapping their wings. Those birds, who have a six-foot wing spread, mind you, apparently tripped up the vassal, delaying him long enough for the lord to reach the safety of Castle Rutledge."

"Goodness. Did your ancestor retaliate against the vassal?"

"No. By dawn, the marquis was well on his way to London. From all accounts, he rarely returned to Castle Rutledge and spent most of his life at his other estates."

"And that is the symbol someone chose to display on your crest?"

"Well, the swans did save his life" —he bit back a smile— "or at least his *membrum virile.*"

"Yes, well. I suppose I should be thankful. If the axe had done its work, you wouldn't be here."

His lips quirked with amusement. "There is that."

"Do swans still reside at Castle Rutledge?"

"Absolutely. The marquis issued an edict they were not to be disturbed. That custom still stands. No one is allowed to harm them even though they can be bloody nuisances at times." He slapped his hands on his thighs and came to his feet. "Now Mister Grant tells me our luncheon is ready to be served. Shall we proceed to the dining room? Cook and her staff have worked very hard on preparing their very best."

I glanced down at my long list with dismay. "We have so many items to discuss."

"We can do that after the meal, can't we?" He held out his hand.

Taking it, I stood. "Yes, of course." It'd be churlish to refuse, especially when the kitchen staff had put forth quite an effort.

As it turned out, the food was indeed wonderful. Robert's cook must have contacted ours at Worthington House, for she'd prepared my favorite dishes—fig and Stilton salad with port wine dressing, beef tenderloin served with a Madeira green peppercorn sauce and accompanied by Lyonnaise potatoes. For dessert, she'd presented us with a floating island comprised of a lemon-scented custard sauce and raspberries. Robert chose a red Bordeaux as his wine of choice. Afterward, I insisted on visiting the kitchen so I could personally thank Cook and indeed everyone who had a role in the meal.

"You enjoyed the luncheon," Robert said as we made our way from the kitchen back to the library.

"It was wonderful, Robert. But I now feel like having a bit of a lie in."

With a glint of humor in his eyes, he offered a suggestion for my predicament. "I have many beds, all of which are at your disposal.

"Including yours, I suppose."

"If you wish. But I recommend we reserve that one for our wedding night."

My cheeks heated up. "You tease. I can't imagine what Mother would say."

Sitting once more on the small sofa, he patted the space to his right, a clear invitation for me to sit next to him. As if I would do anything else.

"Speaking of beds," I fetched my notebook, "Mother suggested a separate bedchamber for me."

His brow wrinkled, but he spoke not a word.

"Hear me out."

"Of course."

"I have an extensive wardrobe which is bound to grow after we marry."

"And you need space to store it. I understand."

"Yes, but that's not the only reason. Mother believes a

lady needs a separate bedchamber for those times she's indisposed." Best keep the conversation as clinical as possible.

"Plan to be indisposed on a regular basis?"

"It's, err, a womanly function."

His brow cleared up. "Your time of the month, you mean?"

My cheeks heated up. "I was trying to be polite."

He cupped my cheek. "No need to, my love. I'm aware that ladies have womanly functions."

I glared at him.

He captured my hands in his own. "Catherine, there is no need for you to sleep in a separate bed during that time. Unless you wish to do so, that is."

I wrinkled my nose. "Would it be horrible of me if I did?"

He flashed a lopsided smile. "Of course not. This will be your home. Our marriage. If you feel such a need, I will neither question nor disapprove of it. I want you to be happy, darling."

"Thank you. That's a weight off my shoulders." I glanced down at the list. "I may need to redecorate, not only my bedchamber, but other rooms."

"You may do so with my blessing, except for my private study. I rather like it as it is."

"I wouldn't dream of changing it." I smiled as I recalled something Mother had done.

"What's so amusing?"

"Mother once added a parrot to Father's study. To keep him company, she said."

His eyes crinkled at the corners. "I gather it did not go well."

"To say the least. Father was on a transatlantic call when the parrot spouted off. He had quite a salty vocabulary."

"He's not still there, is he?"

"No. Mother gifted it to Lady Cargyll. She rather enjoys his scandalous language."

"Your mother possesses a rare gift. The knowledge of knowing what people like."

"That she does."

He glanced around the library. "I'd rather like to keep this room as it is."

"So would I." I loved the book-lined walls, the cozy fire-place, the comfy chairs.

After his gaze finished roaming the space, it landed back on me. "Your birthday is approaching."

"So it is." I'd wondered if he'd remember. Last year my parents celebrated my twenty-first birthday by holding a ball. Although I barely knew Robert at the time, I'd invited him. An excellent decision for we'd enjoyed a magical dance. That's when I started to fall in love with him.

"Any particular way you'd like to spend it?" he asked.

"With you."

"Alone or with company?"

"Supper, followed by cocktails and dancing. Ooh, I know. Let's make it a party. Margaret and Sebastian, Lady Emma and Marlowe, Ladies Mellie and Lily. Ned and Hollingsworth, plus us. That would make it ten."

"What about the Duke of Hanover? Isn't he courting Lady Melissande?"

"He's much too busy with diplomacy to dance attendance on her. Besides, she's cooled on him."

"Very well. I'll arrange it. Will The Ivy for supper and Gennaro's for dancing do?"

"One of the best restaurants and the hottest jazz club in town?" I clutched my hands to my chest. "Be still my heart."

Little did I know that night would have a profound effect on my life.

CHAPTER 3

LADIES OF DISTINCTION DETECTIVE AGENCY

*C*ONDAY, I drove Lady Emma and Betsy, our agency receptionist and my former lady's maid, to the Ladies of Distinction Detective Agency. Located as it was in an impressive townhouse off Hanover Square, our agency couldn't have asked for a better address.

While Lady Emma rushed into her office and Betsy strolled to her desk, I practically danced on air as I made my entrance.

"What has you in such a good mood?" Lady Aurelia, our newest lady detective, asked. Poised on the stairs that led to the higher floors, she had quite the vantage point to my exuberance.

"Robert."

"No!" She teased. We'd hired her several months ago when the business had grown beyond Lady Emma's and my abilities to handle the enquiries. As part of our employment offer, we'd included her living quarters on the townhouse's third floor. She'd proven to be a hardworking, smart, no-nonsense investigator, and a wise hiring choice.

"He's arranging for my birthday celebration. Supper at The Ivy and dancing and cocktails at Gennaro's. Would you like to join us?"

"I thank you, but no. Aside from having two left feet, I prefer to spend my evenings reading a good book, next to a warm fireplace, sipping hot cocoa."

I gazed out the window where the birds were chirping, and the trees were blooming. "It's May."

"And the evenings are still cold."

She had a point. "Very well. But if you change your mind, please let me know."

"I won't. A new Agatha Christie is being published any day now. *The Man in the Brown Suit*. I mean to read it."

"She's a fabulous writer. I read one of her mysteries last year on my way back from finishing school."

"Which one?"

"Ummm, it had *styles* in the title. A murder that took place in a country manor."

"*The Mysterious Affair at Styles*. Her first book."

"That's it! I really enjoyed it. How many has she written?"

"This next one will be her fourth. It won't have Hercule Poirot in it, though." She sounded a bit disappointed. "I have high hopes she'll write more with him in them."

"He's quite a clever detective."

"He is that." She glanced at her watch. "Well, better toddle off. I have an enquiry that won't investigate itself." Unlike her earlier days when she'd dressed in rather dowdy clothing, today she was wearing a fashionable spring coat and carrying a stylish handbag and matching umbrella.

"Which one?" We had so many I barely kept track of my own, never mind hers.

"Lady Carissian. An heirloom brooch has vanished. She suspects one of the maids."

Many of our minor investigations dealt with missing items, mostly jewelry. More often than not, the item had been misplaced. Of course, we never turned down those enquiries. Not only did they bring a handsome income to the agency, but almost always were easily resolved.

"Happy sleuthing!" I said as she sailed out the door.

"Would you like a cuppa, Miss?" Betsy asked, gazing up from her desk. Not only was she our receptionist, but our typist, assistant bookkeeper, and preparer of tea.

"Not at the moment, Betsy. Thank you. But have one if that's what you wish." We'd built a tea station into a cupboard which contained not only an electric kettle but tea, coffee, and sugar. It was so well hidden, no one but us knew it was there.

"Ta, Miss. I'll wait." She pointed to the mountain of paperwork neatly piled next to her.

Once I stashed my cloche and coat in the foyer wardrobe, I walked into Lady Emma's office. Every Monday morning we held a weekly meeting to review open cases, assign new ones, and discuss strategies for moving forward. Usually, it went smoothly, but the expression on her face told me that might not be so today.

"What's wrong?" I asked closing the door behind me.

She rested her clasped hands on the desk. "We have more than enough work to keep us quite busy."

"I know." This was not news.

"Last week Sir Frederick Stone asked us to investigate a new matter."

I nodded. Sir Frederick, who'd represented Robert in the Oxford murder case, had been so impressed with my detective skills, he'd hinted at hiring our agency for future enquiries. To our delight, he'd come through. Mister

Clapham, the former Scotland Yard detective inspector who now worked for us, had taken on the bulk of that work—an investigation into a certain shady character. That meant he was not available for other enquiries as he was tailing the gentleman.

"Taking on Mrs. Worthington's gala responsibilities on top of all the agency tasks is more than I can handle."

"Can I take some of them off your hands?"

"You have more than enough to do, Kitty. We need additional help. I suggest we hire someone."

"Whatever you think is best. But . . ."

"Yes?"

"Well, the gala responsibilities are only temporary."

"Maybe so, but it's my considered opinion Mrs. Worthington needs an assistant. A permanent one. Even as organized as she is, she can't keep up with the flow of work that the chairmanship of the Ladies Benevolent Society requires."

"Couldn't someone in the charity help?"

"I telephoned several of the ladies on the committee and asked them to take on some of the tasks. Simple ones. Nothing too complicated. Telephoning donors and asking for a donation. Visiting the stationer to pick up invitations to the gala. I did not even ask them to address them. I'll do that. Every one said she was too busy with the season to take on additional duties."

I clenched my jaw. "But they're never too busy to claim credit for the Society's success." Last year, the organization had raised sufficient money to fund the Children's Home Orphanage as well as numerous other charities, including Magdalen House, a home for fallen women.

"Mrs. Worthington certainly has much more on her plate than they do. Given her health concerns, she should consider resigning."

"She would never do that. Too many individuals depend on the Society for housing, food, education, their health." But Lady Emma was right. We had to take some of the work off her, and Mother's, plates. "Let's do it. Let's hire someone. What should we require for the assistant qualifications?"

"Someone familiar with office procedures, who can use all modern conveniences."

"Such as the telephone," I suggested.

"And a typewriter. We need the work to be legible."

"We'll need someone who can speak like a lady as well." We wouldn't want someone with a cockney accent telephoning one of the upper crust. Not only would we never hear the end of it, but Mother would find out. And that was something to be avoided at all costs. "But where would we find such a person?"

"Agencies for temporary office workers are starting to open in town," Lady Emma said.

"Really?"

"Yes. I'm sure we can find someone suitable for our efforts. If we include a stipend to cover her room and board, we're sure to have qualified candidates beating down our door."

"Let's do it. Let's start looking. We'll interview them here."

"Should the agency cover her salary?" Lady Emma asked. "It'd be a stretch, but I believe we could manage it."

"No. She wouldn't be a member of our staff. I'll pay it out of my own funds. I'm sure Ned will approve the disbursements." My brother Ned managed my dowry since, under British law, females were not deemed capable of handling their money. He'd never once turned down my requests. I doubted he would deny this one as it would benefit Mother.

"I'm so glad you agree. The gala is two months away. We can offer the person we hire that length a period of work. If she proves capable, we can recommend her to Mrs. Worthington once the event is done."

I sighed. "Then it'll be a matter of convincing Mother."

"Talk to Mr. Worthington. Explain what we've done. He's sure to have some suggestions."

I wrinkled my nose. "I don't know. That's rather under-handed, don't you think?"

"She need never find out."

I laughed. "Oh, Lady Emma. You don't know Mother. She always finds out. I'm sure to feel her wrath once she does. But I won't mind. I'd be doing it for her own good. Let's go ahead with the plan."

That's how we ended up with Marigold Jenkins who turned out to be an excellent hire. She was so efficient we had a hard time keeping her busy with only the gala matters. So, I telephoned Margaret to see if she needed any help. As it turned out, she did. While Ladies Lily and Melissande were perfectly lovely young women, they did not have an orga-nizing bone in their bodies. Most of the work had fallen back on Margaret. Since the invitees to Margaret's fundraiser and the gala tended to be drawn from the same pool of charitable donors, Miss Jenkins took on that task as well. It soon became evident she needed her own telephone line as she tended to do most of her business over that device. So we installed a private one for her.

The only tasks that were performed through handwritten notes were communications through the post with prospec-tive donors. Mother was adamant about that. But Miss Jenkins added a simple statement at the end of each note. If the donor wished to be notified by another method, such as the telephone or by messenger, they could make their wishes known by checking off a box. Although most preferred the invitations themselves be delivered rather than issued by telephone, many chose something other than a handwritten note for more mundane matters.

When it came to working with vendors, however, Miss Jenkins used the telephone. If one proved difficult, she paid a personal visit and resolved the matter.

At our next status meeting, Lady Emma suggested we hire her on a permanent basis. "She's excellent at dealing with vendors. I wouldn't have to chase down clients who haven't paid their fees which would give me more time to handle enquiries."

"That's an excellent suggestion, Lady Emma. But what about Mother and the Ladies Benevolent Society?"

"As efficient as she is, Miss Jenkins could do both. Mrs. Worthington would not suffer. We'd make sure of that. If her duties become too onerous, we could hire additional staff."

"We would need a larger property in that case," I said. "Or maybe lease the space next door. It's been vacant for the last six months. We would need a thruway between the two townhouses, but it should be easy enough to build one."

Lady Emma wrinkled her nose. "That might be more that our budget allows." She performed the accounting duties for the agency and was rather conservative when it came to our bottom line. A good thing for I would have gladly spent the money without paying heed to the consequences.

"Or there might not be a need after all," I offered. "Once the season ends, our business will more than likely diminish."

"I'm not certain about that, Kitty. Sir Frederick hired us to investigate that one matter. And just yesterday another solicitor asked us to take on an enquiry. That's the sort of business that happens year-round."

She was right. Crime certainly didn't keep to the social calendar. Things were not as clear as all that, though. It might be best to adopt a wait-and-see attitude. "How about we defer that decision for a couple of months? We can reassess at that time."

She retrieved the planner she used to keep track of agency matters. "I'll put it on our calendar."

Grateful for her professionalism, I said, "I don't know what I'd do without you, Lady Emma."

Her cheeks grew pink. "Thank you. I love what we're doing with the agency."

I pressed her hands. "It's thriving, in large part thanks to you."

CHAPTER 4

LADY MELISSANDE'S HEARTACHE

*W*E'D BEEN SO BUSY AT THE AGENCY, it was close to six before Lady Emma and I arrived home which meant we had but an hour to bathe and dress before the cocktail hour was announced. But Grace, my lady's maid, was awaiting me in my room. So I'd managed to do so, with more than a few minutes to spare.

I was descending the stairs when I caught the piano renderings of Mozart's *Requiem*. A beautiful composition to be sure, but not one to lift the spirits.

"Lady Melissande?" I asked Carlton who stood sentinel by our front door to welcome our supper guests.

"Yes, Miss."

When something troubled her, she proceeded to the music room to play funeral dirges. Classically trained as she was, her renditions were good enough to be heard at the Royal Albert Hall. Still, requiems tended to grate on everyone's nerves. "How long has she been at it?"

"For the last hour, Miss."

I could see by his expression he was not enjoying the concerto. Not that he'd ever complain.

"Any inkling why she's turned melancholic?"

"The Duke of Andover visited earlier today."

"Ah." The duke and Lady Melissande had what you might call an understanding. An informal wooing arrangement, if you will. The courtship, however, had not proceeded smoothly. His duties as his country's diplomatic envoy had kept him away from almost all of the season's social events, including her come-out ball. Although she hadn't said a word, she'd been sadly disappointed. She had not lacked for suitors. Her beauty drew gentlemen like moths to a flame. But she'd felt constrained, as she was not free to encourage their attentions. Maybe the duke's visit had brought matters to a head. "I'll talk to her. If Mother asks, please let her know I'm in the music room."

"Of course, Miss."

The stroll to that destination gave me time to think about my best approach. I settled on kind, but not inquisitive. That was bound to garner the best response.

"Hello," I said stepping into the room.

She stopped playing as pink bloomed across her cheeks. "Hello."

Poor thing was embarrassed. Well, I couldn't have that. "That was lovely."

"Thank you." She clutched her hands on her lap.

"I understand the Duke of Andover paid you a visit."

She startled but then nodded. "He can't attend the Ladies Benevolent Society Gala. Andover is celebrating its 250th anniversary, and his father requested his presence."

"They've mended their relations," I murmured in amazement. The duke and his father, the former Prince of Andover,

24

had not parted in the best of terms to put it mildly. But seemingly, they'd repaired the breach.

She nodded again. "Now that his grandfather has passed, his father is the new king. His own title has changed. He's now the Prince of Andover and the direct heir to the throne." She sighed. "I wouldn't mind his missing the gala so much. I understand it's something he must do. Except . . ." Tears coursed down her cheeks.

"Except?" I gently prompted as I took a seat next to her on the piano bench.

"He always puts his country ahead of me. Oh, Kitty." She flung herself into my arms.

For several minutes I allowed her grief to flow. To heal, she had to lance the wound. Finally, when the emotional storm diminished, she batted the moisture from her face. "Oh, dear, I must look a fright."

"Here," I fetched the small, lacy handkerchief I'd tucked into my wristwatch. I'd learned to carry one with me at all times.

After employing it, she gazed at me with a watery smile. "Better?"

"Much." Even with a blotchy face, she was still beautiful. "So, when will he return?"

She hitched up her chin. "I haven't the foggiest. I ended things with him."

"Did you really?" Who knew she had it in her?

"You disapprove?" Her defiance faded as her voice wavered.

"Of course not." I hugged her. "You must do what's right for you."

"I was raised away from my family, away from everyone I loved. The nuns at the convent were kind, but I was discouraged from becoming attached to them."

Brought up as I was in the bosom of a loving family, I

couldn't even begin to understand the loneliness she must have felt.

"If I married him, it would be more of the same. He would always put Andover ahead of me, as well he should. I just don't want that for myself. I want a husband who loves me, a family to care for." She came to her feet to wander around the room. "The thing of it is, though, it felt right when I ended it. I'm not so sure now." She turned to me. "Is that awful of me?"

Rising, I placed an arm around her shoulders. "It's bound to unsettle you for a time. After all, you'd planned your future around him."

"I feel unmoored, lost."

I turned her toward me. "You're not lost, Lady Mellie. On the contrary, you just found yourself."

"You think so?" She flashed a brilliant smile.

"Absolutely."

The first gong of the evening sounded.

"Cocktails!" She cheered up at the thought.

"Yes. Now why don't you run upstairs to your room and make repairs. I'll tell everyone you'll be late."

She hugged me. "Thank you, dear Kitty. You're a wonder."

I laughed. "I don't know about that."

Fifteen minutes later, Lady Mellie joined us in the drawing room. She'd not only refreshed her makeup but donned a fresh gown. To say she looked splendid was an understatement.

"Now, what's got you in such a good mood?" Lord Hollingsworth, her brother, asked. More often than not he joined us for supper. So much so Mother no longer issued him an invitation. He was just expected as a matter of course.

"I ended things with the Duke of Andover." The smile on her face never wavered although it must have cost her dearly.

"Did you really?" His brow wrinkled with concern.

"Yes." Her lips wobbled for a moment, and her eyes grew suspiciously moist.

Hollingsworth had never been slow to pick up on people's moods. As close as he now was to his sister, he didn't miss the mark. Gently taking her arm, he led her to a spot near the window far enough from the guests they could conduct a private conversation and would lend her the privacy she needed to regain her composure.

"Would you like another sidecar?" Robert asked, pointing to my now empty cocktail glass.

"Yes, please. That will have to be my last one, though. I don't want to get bosky."

He grinned. "Especially when wine will be served with supper."

While he went off to get my drink, I observed family and guests. Mother and Father were standing by the mantel making polite conversation. Ned and Lady Lily had chosen a sofa to make calf eyes at each other. If those two were not engaged by the end of the social season, I would eat my finest cloche hat.

However, not everyone was in a convivial mood. Marlowe and Lady Emma, seated on an isolated settee on the other side of the room, appeared to be arguing. From her expression, she wasn't too pleased with what he was saying.

"Here you are." Robert handed me the cocktail.

Comprised of cognac, orange liqueur, and lemon juice, a sidecar landed on the tart side. But Robert had sugared the rim which would add a bit of sweetness to the mix. Taking a sip, I voiced my approval, "Perfect. Thank you."

"I aim to please, darling," he said before noticing the gaze I was directing toward the two combatants. "Trouble in paradise?"

"It's never been paradise. Not with those two. I wish, oh, I don't know what I wish."

He raised a questioning brow.

"Marlowe wants her to quit being a lady detective after they marry. If they marry." A thought suddenly occurred to me and I pinned my gaze on him. "You should talk to him. After all, you're perfectly fine with my chosen profession."

He laughed. "Oh, no. I'm not stepping on that hornet's nest. They'll need to reach an agreement on their own, without outside interference."

He was right. Still, I wished I could do something. "They truly love each other, you know. They'd be miserable apart."

"They're miserable together," he rightfully pointed out.

I tossed a glance toward Marlowe and Lady Emma. "Not always. Sometimes she positively glows with happiness. But other instances . . ." I allowed the thought to dangle in the air.

"You can't fix all the ills of the world, Catherine." Robert's gaze was nothing but kind. "Now shall we talk about our honeymoon? We'll need to start making plans."

I pinned a happy grin on my face. "Yes, let's."

He led me to a vacant sofa. "Where would you like to go?"

I didn't have to think about it twice. "Paris." A year ago, Ned had escorted me home from the Swiss finishing school I'd attended. As he had a prospective client to meet at the City of Lights, we'd paused our journey there for one day. I'd visited as many sites as I could. But it hadn't been enough. A honeymoon in Paris would be everything I'd ever dreamed of and more.

He kissed my hand. "Then Paris it shall be."

CHAPTER 5

KITTY'S BIRTHDAY CELEBRATION

*M*Y BIRTHDAY SUPPER AT THE IVY was beyond splendid. Robert had arranged for a private room, a good thing for we ended with fourteen guests. Margaret and Sebastian, of course were there, along with most of our friends, including our newest acquaintances, Lord Salverton and Lady Delphine. We'd enjoyed sausage pinwheels and egg salad and tea sandwiches for appetizers while the soup was pear potato. A scrumptious roast beef was paired with Yorkshire pudding, and for dessert we'd enjoyed a meringue and whipped cream confection mixed with strawberries the restaurant called an Eton mess. It may not have been the neatest treat, but it was certainly delicious. To make it an even more special evening, Robert had a Victrola delivered which played classical music while we ate.

After the meal I was presented with many gifts, everything from a gorgeous jewelry box from Ned and Lady Lily, to a set of journals from Lady Emma and Lord Marlowe who suggested I use them during our investigations. Hollingsworth and Lady Melissande presented me with an atlas so I could always find my way home. I was truly touched. He'd remembered how horrible I was at geography. Lady Delphine's gift was a pair of sky-blue kid gloves, while Lord Salverton's was a cloche hat to replace the one I'd lost as a result of his insane driving. Margaret and Sebastian's gift was a book titled, *A Lady's Guide to Married Life*.

"Is it like a *Lady's Guide to Etiquette and Deportment*?" I asked. "I never managed to finish that one."

"It's written along similar lines," Margaret said. "I book-marked the honeymoon section."

After finding that chapter, I read from it aloud. "Make a regular habit of trimming your toenails. No husband wants to share a bed with a three-toed sloth."

I dissolved into laughter, as did the rest of the group. "I'll make a point of that."

"If you're prone to cold feet, wear stockings. Your spouse will appreciate not encountering ice blocks on his wedding night."

"Oh, my!" Lady Lily exclaimed. "That doesn't seem very romantic."

"Do not eat or drink anything that will cause foul breath. Your beloved will not want to kiss someone who reeks of garlic or onions."

"Now that's just common sense," Lady Mellie said.

I closed the book and placed it on the table. "Thank you, Margaret and Sebastian. I'll read it from cover to cover before my wedding day. Or not."

Everyone laughed.

"However, I'm curious. Is there a gentleman's guide?"

"No." Margaret wrinkled her nose. "I searched."

"Figures."

"Ahem," Sebastian cleared his throat. "As the only married man in this gathering, I'll be glad to share my husbandly advice."

"I bow to your greater wisdom," Robert said, suiting action to words.

Sebastian captured Margaret's hand in his own and tenderly kissed it. "Love her. Simply love her."

Suiting action to words, he tenderly kissed Margaret. All the ladies sighed; Hollingsworth and Marlowe predictably groaned.

While everyone was making suggestions as to what to include in a gentleman's guide, Robert retrieved a jewelry box from his evening coat and handed it to me. "Happy birthday, Catherine."

I opened it to find a pearl bracelet, a pave diamond set in yellow gold in its center. A small gold swan dangled from the clasp. "Thank you, Robert. It's truly lovely." I offered him my lips for a kiss. He didn't disappoint.

"Just so you know," he said, "I'll take you any way you came, my darling, frozen feet and all."

I kissed him again. How could I not love such a man?

As we couldn't travel to our next destination with all my presents, Robert arranged for them to be stowed safely in the manager's office. He would have them safely delivered to Worthington House the next day.

Knowing we'd be drinking wine and cocktails during the evening, we'd opted for taxicabs as our mode of transportation. A party of fourteen might prove a challenge, but Robert had arranged for several which were waiting at the kerb. Laughing gaily, we climbed into them, and soon we were being whisked to the jazz club.

Gennaro's, with vines hanging down the walls and potted greenery dotting the space, resembled an Italian grotto. The club was packed with revelers. Some were kicking up their heels on the dance floor while others sat at tables that lined the walls on opposite sides. At the far end, an American jazz band was playing a ragtime song on the stage.

As Margaret had a particular aversion to cigar smoke, we asked to be seated near a window. If it became too much for her, we could crack it open and allow some fresh air to circulate.

To my surprise, our party of fourteen was shown to an area that had been cordoned off. "However did you manage to reserve so many tables as busy as the club is?" I asked Robert.

An enigmatic grin rolled across his lips. "I know the owner."

Robert would never use his position at Scotland Yard to curry favor. But I could well imagine the proprietor would be eager to remain on the good side of an officer of the law.

Once we ordered our drinks, we settled in to enjoy the fabulous music of the Rhythm Kings jazz band. Originally from Louisiana, its meteoric rise had taken them to Chicago, New York, Paris, and now London.

"Aren't they fabulous?" I asked Robert.

"Absolutely," he answered.

"They never play a musical composition the same way twice," Lady Mellie said. Seated to my right, she must have overheard my comment to Robert.

"Really?"

She nodded. "Improvisation is part of a jazz band's charm."

After our waiter arrived with our cocktails, most of our party was happy to drink and listen to the music. But after a couple of songs, I came to my feet and extended my hand to Robert. "Let's dance, Inspector."

Happy to comply with my request, he led me to the floor

while members of our party who shall remain nameless—Marlowe and Hollingsworth—tossed insults his way.

"We called him two left feet at Oxford, Kitty," Hollingsworth hooted.

"Careful lest he stomp on your toes," Marlowe warned.

I ignored their jibes, mainly because I knew Robert was an expert dancer. As for me, I'd been practicing the Charleston and the Black Bottom with Lady Lily while Lady Mellie played away at the piano. So I was not about to be embarrassed.

We kicked up our heels, twisted our feet, and tossed our arms in the air, laughing gaily all the while. After seeing how easy the dance was, Hollingsworth took to the floor with Lady Delphine and Margaret with Sebastian. Taking pity on Lady Mellie who was bouncing on her chair, Salverton asked her to dance as well. Marlowe and Lady Emma remained at our table. A good thing for someone had to watch our clutches and personal items. Two tunes later, the band announced they were taking a break. Something I appreciated, as I was out of breath.

We returned to our tables to find two gentlemen and a lady talking to Marlowe and Lady Emma, none of whom I recognized. After a quick round of introductions, they wandered off, the lady and one of the gentlemen claiming a need to rejoin their group.

A server stopped by our table with another round of cocktails. Parched as I was, I was immensely grateful.

"Friends of yours, Marlowe?" I asked once I'd taken a sip.

"Not friends exactly, more like acquaintances from Oxford. The gentlemen, I mean. I've never met the lady. Derwent is a loose fish, to tell you the truth. Never has a feather to fly with. More than likely tonight he's sponging off his friend."

I could not ask any more questions as just then the band

returned. Its leader soon introduced their singer, Monique Gautier, a dusky beauty stunning in an embellished sequin ruby gown. As it turned out, she had the talent to match.

Someday he'll come along
The man I love
And he'll be big and strong
The man I love
Then when he comes my way
I'll do my best to make him stay.

Her smoky voice filled the room, mesmerizing all who listened, especially one tawny-haired gentleman seated to the right of the stage who couldn't take his eyes from her. Somehow, she seemed to be singing for him alone.

"That's rather lovely," I whispered to Robert.

He squeezed my hand. "Yes, it is."

He'll look at me and smile, I'll understand
Then in a little while, he'll take my hand
And though it seems absurd,
I know we both won't say a word.

The tawny-haired gentleman raised a glass to her. She acknowledged the toast with an almost imperceptible nod.

He'll build a little home that's meant for two
From which I'll never roam
Who would, would you?
And so all else above I'm dreaming of...
The man...
I...
Love!

When the song ended, there was a moment of silence before thundering applause rained down on her. Miss Gautier stood shyly accepting the accolade. Seemingly, she was not used to such wild approbation. But it was well deserved.

A nattily dressed gentleman climbed the steps on the side of the stage. In his arms, he carried a bouquet of what must have been two dozen red roses. As he presented them to her, he pointed to the gentleman who'd toasted her.

"Goodness! He's really smitten with her," I whispered.

Robert nodded agreeing with me.

"Who is he?" I asked. Maybe someone at our table recognized the gentleman.

Salverton answered. "Lord Rosewood. A friend to the prince."

"Of Wales?"

"Yes." His brow wrinkled.

Was there something about Lord Rosewood's attraction to the jazz singer that troubled him? Interesting, if true. But nothing that concerned me. After all, he was entitled to his private thoughts.

I shifted my gaze back to the stage where Miss Gautier was offering Lord Rosewood a smile. Even as he reciprocated, she returned the bouquet to the gentleman who'd brought them. He walked toward the left and disappeared through a door. More than likely, it led to the backstage area. The roses would need to be put in a vase.

The band struck up once more. This time with a jazzier tune. Proving her range, Miss Gautier was soon lending her amazing voice to the lyrics. But as everyone was enjoying her performance, an altercation broke out between Lord Rosewood and a dark-skinned gentleman whose words were loud enough to be heard above the music.

"I told you to stay away from my sister."

Had to be the singer's brother. Apparently, he objected to her friendship with the aristocrat.

Lord Rosewood raised a brow. "Surely, it's up to Monique to determine who she'd like to spend time with, Mister Gautier."

"She's just turned eighteen. She doesn't know what she wants."

"I disagree, Sir."

Obviously, Rosewood was doing his best to keep things civil.

But it didn't do any good. Gautier's answer was to take a swing at him. Lord Rosewood aptly dodged the blow causing Gautier to lose his balance and land face down on the floor.

Before he could come to his feet, two burly men appeared out of nowhere, yanked Gautier off the floor, and dragged him away.

"That's one way to stop a disagreement," Robert said.

"That young fool hasn't done his sister, or the band, any favors," Salverton chimed in.

"What do you mean?" I asked.

"Word will spread about the argument, especially after the gossip rags get a hold of it. The club owner may very well terminate the band's engagement as it's bound to affect his business."

"Or make the club more popular," Lord Marlowe said with a grin. "Nothing like a fistfight to attract customers."

"You may be right." Sebastian said, coming to his feet. "On that note, we'll be taking our leave. Margaret's feeling the effects of all the cigar smoke."

He had a valid reason for her eyes were red. But more than anything else, I believed they craved privacy. Monday morning Sebastian was leaving for Wynchcombe Castle where he would remain for at least two weeks attending to estate duties. Margaret couldn't accompany him as she was much too busy attending to her good works, fundraising for women's causes, and finishing her last term at Oxford.

My sister kissed my cheek. "Sorry to miss the rest of your birthday celebration."

I hugged her. "No need to apologize, Margaret. Thank you both for joining us."

After she and Sebastian said their goodbyes to the rest of the party, they walked away hand in hand.

"They're lovely," Lady Delphine said, watching their departure.

"That they are."

The band broke into another lively tune, and dancers soon took to the floor, but I was satisfied to simply enjoy being with Robert and my friends. A couple of songs later, the waiter came around for last call. The club would need to stop serving drinks after one thirty or run afoul of the law.

While waiters were delivering drinks, the band took another well-deserved break. After they left, the room grew quieter, although not entirely silent as people were laughing and talking.

And then suddenly, a sharp crack boomed across the room, loud enough to stop all conversation.

Robert bolted to his feet. "That was a gunshot."

"What! No. That can't be."

Two more loud bangs quickly followed. The club erupted into pandemonium as screams filled the room.

"Hollingsworth, Ned," Robert yelled over the panic. "Get the ladies out of here. Now!"

"But Robert," I protested.

He grabbed my shoulders. In a voice I'd never heard from him before, he commanded, "You will go with them. No argument, Catherine."

I nodded.

He turned to Salverton. "Are you carrying your service weapon?"

Nodding, Salverton drew a revolver from the depths of his coat.

What was he doing with a firearm?

As he and Robert rushed toward the back of the club where the shot had come from, Ned grabbed my arm. "Come, Kitty. We have to go."

Lily was clutching him, her eyes big as platters. Marlowe hadn't waited for orders. He was already halfway toward the exit with Lady Emma on one arm and Lady Delphine on the other.

"Where's Mellie?" Hollingsworth asked glancing around. She was nowhere in sight.

"She had to visit the ladies'," Lady Lily yelled over the deafening screams.

Hollingsworth turned to me. "I'll find her. Go with your brother."

"You'll need a female to enter the ladies' room."

"I can do it. Now go." He pushed me toward Ned.

I dug in my heels. Literally.

"Kitty?" Ned asked.

"Get Lily out. I'll be fine."

With a heavy sigh, he wrapped his arm around Lily's shoulders and pushed their way into the crowd, disappearing in seconds.

"You should have gone with them," Hollingsworth said, a frown to his mouth.

"The longer we argue, the longer it will take to find your sister."

"Very well." He grabbed my arm. Together, we fought our way through the panicked throng fleeing the scene. After several minutes, we finally reached the ladies' bathroom. But Lady Mellie wasn't there. He suggested returning to our table. Maybe she'd returned to that spot. But when someone stumbled into me almost knocking me down, he grabbed my arm and led me to the stage, a relatively safe space. Except for the musical instruments and the microphone, it was empty.

From our vantage point, we searched the crowd. I was horrified by what I saw. The stampeding mob was stepping over anyone who had fallen in their frenzy to reach the exit, not caring who got hurt.

"We'll never find Mellie in this madness." Hollingsworth said, frustration clear in his gaze.

I swallowed back my distress. "We'll find her. She'll stand out in her red hair and blue sequined gown."

"There she is." He pointed to a redhead, who stood clutching a table not far from us.

Charging into the melee, we pushed past the numerous bodies to reach Hollingsworth's sister.

"Mellie!" he yelled as we approached, but she did not hear us in the din. Finally reaching her, he grabbed her arm.

She turned and swung a mean right hook at Hollingsworth, catching him just below the cheek.

No wonder. The lady was not Lady Mellie.

CHAPTER 6

CHAOS AT THE CLUB

"TAKE YOUR BLOODY HAND OFF ME!" The redhead yelled, eyes flashing with fury. She was a sight to behold. Almost as tall as Hollingsworth, she had a well-muscled physique. Unusual for a woman to say the least.

"What on earth are you doing?" Lady Mellie! Out of nowhere, she'd materialized to our right.

"I thought she was you," Hollingsworth said by way of apology.

No wonder. The woman and Lady Mellie were redheads, both wearing sparkling blue frocks. From the back they looked exactly the same.

"My apologies," Hollingsworth. He let go of the other woman and grabbed his sister.

Lady Mellie objected. "Wait. We can't leave Lady Charlotte behind."

"I'm fine," the woman, Lady Charlotte presumably, said.

"Where's your escort?" Hollingsworth asked.

"He was supposed to be fetching us drinks. Probably took off as soon as he heard the shots. The worm," Lady Charlotte exclaimed.

"You can't stay here. It's not safe. Come with us," Lady Mellie said.

Lady Charlotte shot a dubious look toward Hollingsworth. "Who's he?"

"My brother," Lady Mellie said. "Lord Hollingsworth."

"At your service, Lady Charlotte," Somehow in the middle of the insanity that surrounded us, Hollingsworth managed to sketch a graceful bow. "Now I suggest we go."

Lady Charlotte hesitated for a brief moment before she said, "Very well."

Hollingsworth wrapped an arm around Lady Mellie and me. I offered Lady Charlotte my free arm. Together we made a rather effective battering ram as we fought our way through the crowd.

If the inside of the club was sheer pandemonium, the outside was only slightly less so. Hollingsworth escorted us to the relative safety of the entrance to an alley before he went in search of a cab. There were few to be had, as everybody was trying desperately to hail one. We couldn't walk home, not as far as we were. And most definitely not in high heels and evening gowns.

Lady Charlotte turned to me, a wondering gaze in her eyes. "You look familiar. Have we met?"

"Not that I recall," I extended my hand. "Catherine Worthington. Everyone calls me Kitty."

"Ahh." A light in her eyes told me she recognized my name. "The lady detective."

I wasn't surprised she knew my reputation given I was regularly featured in the press, next to *scandalous*, and *no better than she should be*. "That's right."

"You're engaged to that Scotland Yard chief inspector. What's his name?"

"Crawford, er, Sinclair."

Her brow wrinkled. "Which is it?"

"Both. Long story. For another time, perhaps."

"Lady Charlotte's uncle is Earl Marsh, Kitty," Lady Mellie said.

"Ahh," I said. Earl Marsh, a luminary in the House of Lords. Unfortunately, a Conservative. He often opposed Sebastian's efforts to help the poor.

"The bane of my existence," Lady Charlotte said. "He dragged me to London to play political hostess for him."

There appeared to be no love lost between Lady Charlotte and her uncle. I wanted to enquire further, but Hollingsworth suddenly reappeared. "Ned and Lady Lily managed to obtain a taxi." Leading the way, he forced his broad shoulders through the throng. When people didn't move, he shoved them aside. To my surprise, Lady Charlotte did as well. We reached the cab to find Ned and Lady Lily fighting off people who wanted to commandeer the hired vehicle. Pulling no punches, Ned was striking several men while Lady Lily was liberally applying a sharp elbow to anyone who came close.

Good heavens! The crowd had turned into a vicious mob.

Wasting no time, I climbed into the front with the cabbie, while the other ladies piled in the back. Hollingsworth and Ned jumped on the car's running boards to the strong objection of the taxi driver. "'Ere, I can't have you damaging me cab."

"If we do, we'll buy you a new one, my good man," Hollingsworth yelled. When yet another ruffian tried to drag him off the running board, he kicked him in the gut. "Now, drive on. Grosvenor Square, if you please."

"Where are we going?" Lady Charlotte asked.

42

I swiveled toward the rear seat. "Worthington House. We'll make sure you get home safe. Where do you live?"

"Chester Square."

"That's not far from us." I offered a smile to reassure her. Not that she noticed. She was too busy staring at Hollingsworth, a sight to behold with his windblown hair. I imagined that's the way he looked while captaining his tall ship.

"So, that's your brother," she said to Lady Mellie.

"Yes."

"He doesn't seem the usual type." A calculating look in Lady Charlotte's eye seemed to be weighing and measuring Hollingsworth.

"Oh, he's not a dandy, if that's what you mean. He's an explorer. His last expedition took him to the South Seas."

"He sails?" Lady Charlotte asked a note of admiration in her voice.

Lady Mellie nodded. "He has his own ship, the Calypso. He and his crew go exploring every two years or so."

"Really?" Lady Charlotte sat back, but her gaze never left Hollingsworth.

It took twenty minutes or so to reach Worthington House. As we still had to escort Lady Charlotte home, we asked the cab driver to wait, promising generous compensation if he did. He seemed to agree to our suggestion because he turned off the cab's motor.

Carlton, our family butler, was waiting for us at the door. "Miss Worthington. We'd grown concerned." The royal we, of course, as he was the only staff member in sight. "Is everything as it should be?" he asked.

"As much as it can be. I gather you've heard about the unfortunate event at the jazz club?" An understatement. But until we learned more about what had occurred, I couldn't describe it as anything else.

He nodded. "Lady Emma and Lord Marlowe informed us. They await you in the drawing room."

"Thank you, Carlton. We have a guest, Lady Charlotte. One of the gentlemen will escort her home after she catches her breath."

"Of course. Your outer garments?" He inquired.

"I'm afraid they didn't make it." We would have to return for them, of course. When was anybody's guess.

We made our way to the drawing room where Lord Marlowe and Lady Emma had been waiting anxiously for our arrival. Well, she was. He'd seemingly been soothing his nerves with a dram of whiskey, as he had a glass filled with an amber liquid in his hand.

"Lady Delphine?" I asked.

"We escorted her home," Marlowe answered after taking a sip.

"What about Inspector Crawford—I mean Sinclair—and Salverton?" Lady Emma asked.

At some point, we would all stop stumbling over Robert's name change. Just not today.

"Didn't see them again. No doubt we'll discover what happened in the morning." Although concerned, I wasn't worried about his well-being. No more shots had been fired after those initial three. At least none that I'd heard.

The telling of what we'd experienced did not last long. As it was by now close to three, everyone was eager to seek their beds.

The question then became who would escort Lady Charlotte home. As a young lady couldn't very well be seen alone with a gentleman, Lady Mellie volunteered to accompany her brother. He would bring back his sister after Lady Charlotte had been safely delivered to Marsh House. Marlowe declined to join them. He wanted to clear his head, and he lived close enough to walk home.

I sent off Ladies Emma and Lily to seek their slumbers while I stayed up to wait for Lady Mellie. It was not until close to four that I finally gained my bed.

IT SEEMED like I'd barely gotten any sleep when I was being shaken awake. "Kitty, dear."

I blinked to find Mother hovering over me. "What time is it?" The light streaming through the window told me it was not early morning.

"Nearly eleven. Something happened at the jazz club?"

Recalling the events of the previous night, I sat up in a rush. A mistake for it set my head spinning. The result of drinking too many cocktails. Squinting, I said, "Yes. How did you know?"

"It's in the papers, dear." She held out a glass of water and two aspirins. "Drink all the water. It will help. Grace will be along soon with coffee. We'll hold luncheon for you."

I drank two cups of the brew while I bathed. It helped immensely with the headache. Close to noon, I made my way to the drawing room where I found Ladies Lily, Mellie, and Emma, and, of course, Mother. All wore glum expressions on their faces.

"How bad is it?" I asked.

"Bad," Lady Emma volunteered. "Lord Rosewood is dead from shotgun wounds. Maurice Gautier has been arrested."

The singer's brother. "By Robert?"

"Apparently," Lady Emma said.

We didn't have an opportunity to hold a discussion as Carlton soon announced luncheon was served. As we made our way to the dining room, I asked Mother, "Where's Father?"

"He won't be joining us. He had to attend to something at the office."

It was rare that Father worked on Saturdays, but not unheard of. Still, I felt compelled to say, "Nothing serious, I hope."

"He didn't say."

By mutual silent agreement, we steered away from the subject of Lord Rosewood's death during the meal. No one wanted to discuss the macabre topic while we ate.

When the conversation turned to Lady Charlotte, I asked Mellie, "How did you meet her?"

"We were at the modiste one day waiting to be fitted for evening gowns. Somehow the dressmaker's assistants mixed them up. While we waited for them to straighten up the misunderstanding, we chatted."

"I haven't noticed her at any of the balls," I said. Not that I'd attended many of them. As busy as I was with the agency, I'd missed more than half.

"She only attends some of them," Lady Mellie said.

"Any particular reason?" I asked. Lord Marsh's niece would most certainly be invited to most social events.

"She never really explained. But from certain comments she made, I gathered she only attends those issued by hostesses whose husbands have a strong political bent. Her uncle is highly involved in conservative circles. She'd rather be at Marsh Castle, but Lord Marsh threatened to withhold her allowance if she didn't come to town during the social season. He's a widower, so he needs her to act as his social hostess for all the suppers he holds."

"How very odd he entertains so often," I said. As a general rule, widowers did not. They tended to conduct their social activities at their gentleman's clubs, or at events to which they were invited.

"He would like to become the next Lord High Chancellor," Mother said. "As that position is appointed by the Crown, he needs to wine and dine those who have the king's ear, as well as the prime minister's."

Trust Mother to be thoroughly knowledgeable as to matters involving Parliament and the Crown.

"Is there a particular reason why Lady Charlotte prefers Marsh Castle to London?" I asked.

"She enjoys cruising the river Exe," Lady Mellie said. "Apparently, she's an excellent sailor."

I almost choked on a grape. No wonder she showed such an interest in Hollingsworth. "That's . . . interesting."

"Her brother's estate is located in Exeter, close to the river. Not only does she own a motorboat but also loves to row. She would like to participate in the next Exeter Rowing Regatta. Unfortunately, no women are allowed membership in the rowing club."

"No wonder she has such a strong right hook," I murmured.

"And how did you discover that, Kitty?" Mother asked.

I explained what happened last night ending with, "Next time we see Hollingsworth, he's bound to be sporting a shiner. She apologized later on, of course."

"Ummm," Mother murmured, a gleaming light in her eyes.

Oh, no! She was pairing Hollingsworth with Lady Charlotte. But that would never do. He was a confirmed bachelor. "No, Mother."

She frowned at me. "Whatever are you talking about, Kitty?"

I heaved out a sigh. She'd never admit her matchmaking interest had been piqued. In an attempt to change the subject, I said, "It's almost one. You think we'd have heard from Robert by now."

"I expect we will," Mother said. "Once he has a free moment, that is."

Just as we were finishing our meal, a footman entered and whispered something to Carlton who announced, "Pardon me, Mrs. Worthington. Lord Robert has arrived."

Finally!

CHAPTER 7

AN UNPLEASANT REVELATION

"PLEASE SHOW HIM IN," Mother said.

And then there he was. As always, he was immaculately attired. But there were dark circles under his eyes. Chances were he didn't get much sleep last night.

I walked toward him and curled my arm around his. "Come sit by me."

He shook his head, even as his gaze took me in. "I can't stay. I only came to deliver the news. I knew you would be anxious to hear."

But Mother was having none of his excuse. "Have you had your luncheon?"

He pried his gaze off me long enough to answer, "Haven't had the time, Ma'am."

"Then you must join us. Surely, taking a half hour to eat won't make a difference to your investigation."

I grinned at him. "It won't do any good to argue with Mother, you know. Her mind's quite made up."

One corner of his lips lifted. "Very well. Thank you, Ma'am."

I led him to the spot where a footman had already set a place for him at the table. Since our luncheons were served buffet style, I took his plate and filled it with two helpings of the Quiche Lorraine. On another, I piled the stilton and fig salad before placing the food in front of him.

As it would not do to ply him with questions while he ate, we ladies engaged in desultory conversation about fashion and such. Finally, when he was done with his serving of raspberry meringues, he addressed the issue which had brought him to Worthington House, "I trust you've already heard the details."

"It was in the papers," I said. "Lord Rosewood was killed. How tragic."

"Indeed."

"You arrested Maurice Gautier. The singer's brother?" I asked.

"Yes. It was his revolver, and he was found standing over the body. Although . . . "

"Yes?" I prompted.

"He claimed he was in the club's back alley when the shots were fired."

"Did anybody see him there?"

"No. But we're still doing our enquiries."

"And yet you arrested him."

His steely-eyed gaze focused on me. "It was his gun. He'd been seen arguing with Rosewood. I would not have been doing my duty if I hadn't brought him in." His gaze softened. "He hasn't been charged, Catherine, only detained. It gives me time to investigate." He glanced at his watch. "I hate to eat and leave, but . . ."

"Duty calls," I finished for him.

He nodded.

After he said his goodbyes to Mother and the other ladies, I accompanied him to the front door.

While the footman went to fetch his coat and hat, he said, "You'll be wanting to retrieve your wrap from the club."

I would hate for it to be mislaid. It had been especially designed by Angelique herself to match the red gown I'd worn last night. "We all do." I nodded toward the dining room. The other ladies' outer garments had been left behind as well.

"They're safe. We assigned a police officer to guard the coatroom. No one has access to the club while we investigate."

"I'm in no rush."

"Be that as it may, you'll be able to retrieve them tomorrow. I'll leave word you're to be allowed entrance to the venue."

"When will the club reopen?"

"Not for several days, I imagine. The mad exit caused quite a bit of damage."

"The owner must not be happy about that."

"He's furious about his loss of income as you can imagine."

"Marlowe conjectured the notoriety would draw even more people to the club. Chances are he'll recoup his losses."

"Human nature being what it is, Marlowe's more than likely right. People will want to see where Lord Rosewood was murdered."

After the footman returned with Robert's coat and hat, I dismissed him. I wanted more private time with my fiancé as I had something to say. "I want you to get some rest."

Robert tweaked my chin, a loving gesture he often employed with me. "May I remind you I have a cot in my office?"

As charming as he was, I was not about to give in. "Which is no place to sleep. Promise me you'll go home tonight."

He sucked in a breath. "Catherine, I may not—"

I tugged his silk tie to let him see I was serious. "Promise me."

"Without question, you are the most . . ."

I hitched up a brow.

"Beautiful, persuasive, young lady I've ever met."

I offered him a soft smile.

"Very well, my darling. I promise."

I curled my arms around his neck and drew him closer to me. "See? That wasn't so hard."

He showed his appreciation by thoroughly kissing me, leaving me boneless, breathless, and in desperate search of my next thought.

After he walked out the door, I joined the ladies in the drawing room where they were discussing the murder, sans Mother, who'd retired to her bedroom for her doctor-prescribed rest.

"Do you think Mister Gautier murdered Lord Rosewood, Kitty?" Lady Mellie asked.

"His argument with Lord Rosewood provides motive. The weapon was his. But he claims he was in the club's back alley."

"Surely the alley can't be far from the scene of the crime," Lady Emma said.

"We don't know where exactly Rosewood was killed," I reminded her. "And the entire band was, more than likely, in the backstage area. Anyone could have done it."

"Surely, no one else had motive," Lady Lily pointed out.

"That we know of," I said. "We've investigated enough murders to know motives aren't always clear."

"Could Miss Gautier have killed him?" Lady Mellie asked.

"I don't think so," I replied after thinking it over. "She

seemed smitten with Lord Rosewood." Eager to change the subject, I said, "Robert said we may retrieve our wraps and such tomorrow. In the meantime, they're safe in the club's coatroom. A police officer has been assigned to keep everything secured."

"Well, that's good to hear. My cape was a birthday gift from my brother," Lady Mellie said.

"We can head over to the club after church tomorrow, if that suits everyone."

"Should we invite Lady Charlotte to come along with us?" Lady Mellie asked. "It would allow us to become better acquainted."

"Oh, yes, let's," Lady Lily happily seconded. "And Lady Delphine as well."

We decided on adding a lunch invitation as Mother loved nothing more than a house full of guests. We could head to the club after the meal. Lady Delphine readily accepted once we telephoned. Lady Charlotte could not make the luncheon, but she would love to join our excursion to the club. We arranged to swing by after the meal and pick her up.

THE NEXT DAY luncheon was a rousing success. Not only were the ladies present, but so were Ned and Hollingsworth. Ned always attended Sunday meals. Not only because he was part of the family, but so he could enjoy Lady Lily's company. We never had to invite Lord Hollingsworth. He was an amusing conversationalist as well as Lady Mellie's brother. Unfortunately, Robert had not been able to join us, as he was busy with the investigation. But I held hope I would see him that afternoon at Gennaro's.

Once we finished eating, we piled into Hollingsworth's and Ned's motorcars and headed to Marsh House. Upon our arrival, we were shown to the drawing room where we assumed Lady Charlotte was waiting for us. She was. But so was Lord Marsh.

"Please take a seat. I have something to say." The disapproving expression on his face did not seem to welcome us. Just the contrary. Still, Hollingsworth and I did as he asked.

Lady Charlotte had been relegated to a corner of the room, the vibrant light that shone two nights before now quite dimmed.

What on earth was going on?

"I understand you were of assistance to my niece Friday night." Lord Marsh remained standing.

"Yes," I said. "We were happy to help when—"

He didn't allow me to finish. "I thank you for bringing her safely home. However, as I'm sure you will understand, she will not be furthering your acquaintance. I fear if she does her virtue would be called into question."

"I beg your pardon," I said. Did he mean our association would sully Lady Charlotte? How dare he?

She seemed equally affronted. "Uncle, that's downright rude." That's as far as she got. One quelling glance from him silenced her.

"Miss Worthington, you have to admit that you court notoriety," Lord Marsh declared. "Why, your name is synonymous with scandal, usually attached to a murder. My niece can't afford to have her name dragged though the proverbial mud."

Hollingsworth jumped to his feet. "That's enough, Marsh. Apologize to Miss Worthington."

Lord Marsh raked a disapproving gaze over Hollingsworth whose cheek had turned blue and purple from Lady Charlotte's well-aimed punch. "Do you really feel you're in a position to stand up to me, Hollingsworth? When you come tin cup in hand begging for lucre for your scandalous travels in the South Seas?"

"I'm an explorer, sir."

"Come Hollingsworth. I know what goes on in that part of the world. Licentious behavior, unclad women." His upper lip curled with derision. "Cannibalism."

Hollingsworth stomped forward to tower over Lord Marsh, whose unimpressive five ten height was no match to Hollingsworth's six two.

But it wouldn't do to come to fisticuffs. Lady Charlotte was bound to pay the price.

I grabbed my friend's arm. "Come, Hollingsworth. This will not do any good."

The tension in his arm lessened. He turned to Lady Charlotte and bowed. "Milady."

And then he stomped out with me following close behind.

Of course, when we climbed into the motorcar, everyone had questions, especially Lady Mellie. "Where's Lady Charlotte?"

"She's not coming," I said. "I'll explain later."

The thunderous expression on Hollingsworth's face did not encourage more questions.

CHAPTER 8

AN EXPLORATION AND DEDUCTIONS

*A*T FIRST, WE WERE TURNED AWAY FROM GENNARO'S. But as soon as I explained I was Inspector Sinclair's fiancée and he'd given permission for us to retrieve our things, we were allowed entrance.

Unfortunately, Robert was not there. A disappointment. Not only did I wish to see him, but I had more questions about the investigation. His absence, however, didn't dampen my interest. Just the opposite. He might not be available, but the space was there to be explored. Putting action to thought, I asked Lady Emma to retrieve my wrap while I headed toward the rear where the murder had taken place.

Last time I'd seen the ballroom, a few of the vines had been torn off the walls. Some revelers, emulating *Tarzan of the Apes*, had swung from them to reach the exit. Tables and chairs had been overturned and broken. Doors had been torn off their hinges. The club staff was trying to put everything to rights, but they still had a long way to go.

The door to the backstage area was not locked, so I was able to make my way into it. It was downright eerie how quiet it was, a sharp contrast to the screams that had filled the club when shots rang out almost forty-eight hours ago.

A door to my immediate right begged to be examined. Located as it was directly beneath the stage, it was bound to be a storage area and not a place where people congregated. But I had only a brief time to satisfy my curiosity, so I gave it a pass. For now.

My instincts proved me right as a walk down the hall led me to a cordoned off area. A shiver ran down my spine as I spotted telltale bloodstains on the floor. Had to be where Lord Rosewood had been murdered. Since the last thing I wanted was to dwell on that image, I wandered farther and encountered another door.

Opening it, I recognized the space as the lounge where performers gathered prior to and in between performances. Situated within were one sofa and several chairs, neither fancy, nor elegant, but then they didn't need to be. A makeshift bar that held half-empty whiskey and gin bottles as well as several glasses that needed a good wash was located to the right.

Three doors stood side by side at the rear. One led to a dressing room. Seemingly for the male musicians, as only gentlemen's clothing occupied the space. The next door opened into a bathroom. The last room proved the most interesting of all.

It had been occupied by a woman, as it contained a vanity table, where an expensive makeup collection, a silver hairbrush, and a Chanel No. 5 bottle rested. A simple cot was there as well. Two evening frocks as well as a day dress hung from a clothes rack. The gowns—one blue, one gold—had been fashioned from the finest silks. The red and white day dress bore the Chanel label on its under slip. Nothing cheap for Miss Gautier, for it had to be her changing room. One had to wonder how she could afford such expensive clothes, perfume, and personal items as her singer's salary would, more than likely, not cover their cost.

"Kitty? Where are you?" Lady Emma's voice reached me from a distance.

"I'm in the dressing room. In the back," I yelled.

Her clicking heels echoed until she appeared at the lounge's entrance. "There you are! We're ready to leave." She gazed around. "Did you discover anything?"

"You might say so. I'll tell you about it after we reach home."

THAT NIGHT, we had a full contingent of guests for supper. Even Robert had managed to pry himself away from Scotland Yard long enough to attend. As it turned out, not for a good reason.

"The investigation into Lord Rosewood's death has been reassigned."

"Why?" I asked. We'd settled into the burgundy Chesterfield sofa in the far corner of the drawing room to enjoy the cocktail hour. It provided us with a fair amount of privacy where we could discuss any and all subjects.

A small smile lifted the edge of his well-shaped mouth. "Let's just say I didn't agree with the desired action."

"In other words, they wanted you to charge Mister Gautier with murder, and you refused."

He sipped whiskey from his glass. "Something along those lines."

"So who did the superintendent attach to the case?"

"Chief Inspector Bolton."

I frowned. "Not Scotland Yard's best."

"Ummm."

Of course, he would never denigrate another inspector's name, but nothing prevented me from doing so. Inspector Bolton, who'd investigated the former Duke of Wynch-combe's murder, had missed a vital clue which thankfully Robert had caught. Due to his diligence, the true killer had been exposed.

"Did you uncover any substantial evidence before the matter was handed over to Inspector Bolton?"

"Not substantial, but there was one thing that struck me as odd. The club owner said there was only one entrance from the alley into the backstage area. But I discovered another one in the storage room, a vast space located directly beneath the stage. They keep broken furniture there, as well as other odds and ends."

That must have been the door I noticed but did not enter, as I was more interested in the lounge than anything else. "Maybe he forgot about it."

"Maybe so." His gaze took on a faraway look. "Still, it made me wonder."

"Did you find anything of importance there?"

"No." His glance snapped back to me. "But then I did not investigate it thoroughly. My focus was on interviewing those who were backstage during the shooting."

"Did anybody see who fired the gun?"

"No. The musicians were in the lounge, enjoying their drinks and cigars when they heard the shots. None emerged to investigate."

"Well, that makes sense. I wouldn't be eager to do so, either. What about Miss Gautier?"

"She was upset at the disagreement between her brother and Lord Rosewood. So she retired to her private room to lay down."

She must have done so on the cot I'd spotted in her

dressing room "What did the musicians do when they heard the shots?"

"They barricaded the door with a chair. Some hid in their dressing room, others ran to the bathroom, presumably to escape through the window. But it was too small for any of them to fit through."

I rested my hand on his chest. "Not everyone is as brave as you and Salverton to run toward gunfire."

"It's my job to keep the peace."

"And Salverton?" I'd wondered about him from the time I'd met him. The fact he had a service weapon on his person meant he had something to do with the government. The question was which branch?

All I got in return was a raised brow. Robert would never tell. Taking another tack, I asked, "Who was in the lounge?"

"All the band members and Miss Gautier."

"What about her brother?"

"He claimed he'd been in the alley. After his altercation with Lord Rosewood, he was removed from the club. So he made his way around the back. He was eager to talk to his sister, so he cracked open the door and waited for the band to take their next break. After he heard the music stop, he gave it a few minutes for the band to make their way to the lounge. He was just about to step into the back hallway when he heard the shots. Afraid for his sister, he thrust open the door and ran in. Around the corner, he found Lord Rosewood's body. That's where Salverton and I found him holding the revolver. His, as we later discovered."

"Where did he keep it?"

"In a gun case located inside a cabinet in the dressing room. He claimed he'd locked it away, but I found the gun case open. There were some scratches on the lock, but it did not appear to have been forced."

"Kitty, dear!" Mother, demanding my attention. "Carlton has announced supper."

"Yes, of course." I had more questions, but they would have to wait.

Rising to his feet, Robert extended his hand. I took it and together we followed everyone into the dining room.

After supper ended, Mother reminded me future hostess duties would require me to mingle with my guests. So, I should stop monopolizing my fiancé.

When the gentlemen joined the ladies, I tossed him a rueful smile. He nodded and headed toward Hollingsworth and Ned who were discussing steam propulsion engines, of all things.

I may have been momentarily stymied from further conversation with Robert, but I was not about to give up. We would have other opportunities to discuss Lord Rosewood's murder.

CHAPTER 9

MONIQUE GAUTIER

*M*ONDAY MORNING, Ladies Emma, Aurelia, and I were reviewing our cases in my office when the agency's doorbell rang. After suffering through numerous unwanted intrusions from the press, we'd learned to lock our front door.

Betsy being the closest to the entrance, rushed to open it. After the briefest of pauses, she asked, "May I help you?"

A female voice that spoke with a foreign accent said, "I would like to speak to Catherine Worthington, if you please."

I may not have heard her speak, but I knew who she was. Her speaking voice was as sultry as her singing one.

Still, Betsy had no clue as to her identity "May I have your name, please?"

"Monique Gautier. It's a rather urgent matter."

"One guess what she wants from you," Lady Emma said.

"It wouldn't be a guess," I said. "Let's finish this later."

Ladies Emma and Aurelia sauntered away, leaving me to

greet the lady which I was more than happy to do. "Miss Gautier, I'm Catherine Worthington. Please come in."

Once she stepped into the foyer, I asked if we could take her outer garments, but she preferred to keep them on.

"Would you like some tea or coffee, Miss Gautier?" Betsy asked.

She directed a warm smile toward Betsy. "Coffee would be lovely. Thank you."

After escorting her to my office, I offered her the seat Lady Emma had vacated. A Queen Anne style armchair upholstered in dark rose, the matching one to my own.

While we waited for Betsy to bring the brew, I engaged her in polite conversation. "I enjoyed your singing, Miss Gautier. You have a beautiful voice."

"You've heard me?"

"I was at Gennaro's Friday night."

Her face dropped. "You saw what happened then."

I nodded.

"My brother did not . . . kill Lord Rosewood. He's not a violent man."

All evidence to the contrary. "He argued with Lord Rosewood."

"Arguing with someone is not the same as killing him."

Betsy entered with a tray that held cups and saucers, the coffee service, and a plate piled high with biscuits. After placing it on a side table I kept in my office for that purpose, she left closing the door behind her.

After one sip, Miss Gautier wrinkled her nose at the coffee, but she seemed to enjoy the biscuits. "These are lovely."

"Thank you. They're delivered daily from a tea shoppe down the street."

"They remind me of beignets. Mémère used to bake some for breakfast every morning."

"Where are you from, Miss Gautier?" I knew the state but not the city, although I could have an educated guess.

"New Orleans. That's in Louisiana." She sighed heavily. "I miss it. Miss my friends."

"What about your family?"

"Maurice is the only family I have. Mémère passed away two years ago. That's when he decided I should go on the road with him."

"What's his position with the jazz band?"

"He handles security. That's why he owns a gun. It can be rather dangerous for Negro musicians."

"He seems very protective of you."

"He has to be!" she said with feeling. "Some men think they can take whatever they want."

"Did that happen to you?" I asked as kindly as I could.

She nodded. "Back in New Orleans. I was singing at a club. I've always loved to sing. In church when I was little. At parties when I was older. Someone heard me at one of them, a man who owned a club near the bayou. He wanted to hire me. Mémère refused, but we needed the money. You see, she was sick. So one night, I sneaked out. I went there and sang my heart out. The coins I earned helped to pay for her medicine. At first, it was fine. But then the men started wanting more from me. I was fifteen at the time. One of them caught me one night. He tried"—she swallowed hard—"he tried . . ."

I reached out and covered her trembling hands with my own. "You don't have to explain. I understand."

"That's the last time I sang at the club. Mémère died six months later. Maurice gave away most of her things, sold her house and took me on the road with him. He didn't intend for us to ever return."

"That must have been a difficult thing to accept."

"It was. But he said we should look to the future. And that

was not in New Orleans, but in New York and Chicago. That's where my voice could be heard."

Maurice had been right. "Were you always a singer with the Rhythm Kings jazz band?"

She shook her head. "They had one. I helped with her clothes and things. Picked up after the boys. Somehow, we made it work. We traveled first to Chicago and then New York. That's when Orletta, the singer, got sick. Pneumonia. When she came out of the hospital, she couldn't sing anymore. They couldn't find a replacement, so they asked me. I had to tell everyone I was eighteen so the band wouldn't get into trouble."

"How old are you now?"

"Eighteen."

When I held up a questioning brow, she said, "That's the truth this time."

"How long were you in New York?"

"Six months. Met some great musicians. Reconnected with old friends. Louis Armstrong. You heard of him?"

"Can't say I have."

"If you ever get a chance, go listen to him. That man can play the trumpet like no one else. I swear he makes up notes I've never heard."

"I'll make a note of that." After I realized what I'd just said, we both laughed.

"You're a nice person, Miss Worthington. Better than most people of your class."

"Thank you" was the only thing I could say. But it was time to address the present. "Tell me about Lord Rosewood."

Tears flooded her eyes. "He is"—her breath hitched—"was lovely."

"Where did you meet him?"

"Paris. We were playing at a small club. One night he showed up with a couple of friends. The next he came by himself. The night after that, he sent me two dozen red roses. The note that accompanied the bouquet was lovely—'To the rarest rose of them all.' He signed the card 'George.' It was weeks before I discovered he was a titled lord."

Most men would have bragged about it to secure her favors. But he'd hidden his true identity from her. I wondered why. "Did your brother object to Lord Rosewood in Paris?" More than likely he did. Still, I had to ask.

A small nod. "He warned me away from him. At first, I obeyed his wishes. Stage Johnnies are only after one thing as I have good cause to know. But George was different. He showed up every night without asking anything from me. The club owner claimed he had no idea as to George's true identity, but he deemed him a gentleman of worth and set aside a table for him every night. Apparently, George raised the class of his clientele. He was right. Soon, more guests with fat purses started coming to the club just to hear me sing. Turned out George had been spreading the word about the superb chanteuse at the club. When the club owner extended our engagement, Maurice stopped objecting to George, and I was finally allowed to enjoy a private supper with him."

"And how did that go?"

"He arranged to have it at his apartment. He was a perfect gentleman. All we did was talk while I enjoyed the best meal of my life. French cuisine is superb."

"Yes, it is."

"So how long were you in Paris?"

"Six months. We left about two weeks ago."

"Why?"

"The Summer Olympics. We were staying at a guest house. Our landlord informed us he was tripling our rent for three months—June, July, and August. Apparently, he expected people to flood Paris ahead of the event and remain a month after. We couldn't afford it, so our band leader accepted the engagement at Gennaro's which was to last until the end of June. With the band having gained a bit of fame, clubs from other European cities had reached out to him as well. We are scheduled to travel to Vienna in early July."

"Why did your brother turn against Lord Rosewood again?"

"The band had become successful, so he no longer saw a need for me to favor George with my company."

"You did not agree."

"No." She wiped a tear from her cheek. "I was in love with him, you see."

Not hard to see why she'd fallen for the aristocrat. He'd been quite handsome. And then there was the allure of his title and the fortune he'd seemed to have. But had he loved her? An affair was one thing, but love was another thing altogether.

"I can see the question in your eyes, Miss Worthington. Did Lord Rosewood love me?"

I didn't try to deny it. "You're very perceptive, Miss Gautier."

"Mémère taught me to be. Too many times people say one thing but believe something else. That's how I know I wasn't just a fling to George. I could see it in his eyes, hear it in his voice, feel it in the way he touched me. Like I was the most precious thing in the world to him."

"If I decide to take on this investigation, this agency will incur expenses. To begin with, we would require a retainer. And your brother will require legal representation. Will you be able to afford it all?" A fair question, and one I asked of all clients who sought to retain the agency's services.

She didn't hesitate for a second. "Yes. You see, George settled a sum on me."

CHAPTER 10

LADY EMMA OBJECTS

"YOU CAN'T TAKE ON THIS INVESTIGATION, Kitty, not as busy as we are," Lady Emma said, her mouth set in a stern line.

After Miss Gautier left, I'd stepped into Lady Emma's office to tell her about my conversation with the singer. The last thing I expected was Lady Emma's objection. After all, we'd already obtained additional assistance. "We hired Marigold Jenkins to manage the gala and help with Margaret's fundraiser. And she's also taken on some of the agency's duties."

Her pinched mouth gave no quarter. "That will work for some things, Kitty, but not the high-level management of the agency. Someone must mind the business while you're investigating this matter."

Those last words took me aback. "The reputation of the Ladies of Distinction Detective Agency was built on my murder investigations. Surely, that qualifies as *minding the business*." I couldn't help my waspish tone.

Her raised brow seemingly took umbrage to my statement. "Surely, you mean *our* investigations. You wouldn't have been able to solve all those murders without the assistance of your family and friends."

Heavens! She was really upset. I couldn't respond in a like manner. I would need to tread lightly before this discussion spun out of control. "Yes, of course, it's been a team effort. I didn't mean to intend otherwise." I reached out to hold her hand. "Dear Lady Emma, I don't want us at odds. You're not only my business partner, but a dear friend."

"Am I your business partner, Kitty? The way things stand, I'm only an employee of the firm. And so are you, for that matter."

Well, that took me by surprise. "Whatever do you mean?"

"The Ladies of Distinction Detective Agency was legally organized as a sole proprietorship under your brother's name."

"He thought it best to establish the agency in that manner. As a twenty-one-year-old female with no experience, I couldn't have leased this building, never mind operate a detective agency if the entity belonged to me."

"But things have changed, Kitty. You said it yourself. In the last year our names have been recognized, both by the government and the press, as instrumental in solving several murders. Surely, we can make some changes."

I'd been perfectly happy with the way things stood, mainly because I hadn't given it much thought. But Lady Emma had a point. Maybe it was time to manage the agency in a different way. "I'll talk to Ned. Now, how would you like to proceed?" Clearly, Ned and I couldn't make any decisions without her input. Moving forward, she had to be part of the discussion.

"Well, for starters, we should set up the agency as a partnership, with you and me as the two principals."

"That shouldn't be a problem." At least I hoped it wouldn't be. "What else?"

For the next hour, we discussed her ideas and mine. By the end, we had a working proposal I would make to my brother.

"He's bound to change some things, you know," I cautioned.

"I expect he will since he's much more knowledgeable about the legalities than either of us are. Why don't you set up a meeting we can both attend? That way all our questions can be asked and answered at that time."

"How about I telephone him right now and set something up?" Luckily, Ned was not only in his office at Worthington & Son but free to talk. After I explained what Lady Emma and I wanted to do, there was a momentary silence at his end.

"It's not going to be a problem, is it?" I asked somewhat anxiously.

"Ummm, it depends."

Well, that didn't sound as promising as I'd hoped for.

"I'll need to look into it, Kitty. It'll take a week or so given everything I have on my plate. Will that do?"

"Of course. We'll await your telephone call then."

"Well?" Lady Emma asked as soon as I ended the conversation.

I relayed what Ned had said.

"At least he didn't say no," she said.

"No, he didn't." But then Ned wouldn't. He'd examine the issue, come up with several options to give us what we wanted, and then offer the best solution. "If there's any way to create a partnership between two lady detectives, he'll figure it out. Now what shall we do about the Maurice

Gautier case?"

"We'll have to rearrange things."

"Such as?"

"Lady Aurelia will need to take on the solicitor's matter."

"She won't mind."

"It will require her to talk to some of the chancier elements of society."

"You think she can't handle it?"

Lady Emma grinned. "On the contrary. I think she'll enjoy it so much she'll beg for more of those types of cases."

"And that's a problem?"

"What will you and I do for entertainment?"

I laughed. "Oh, Lady Emma. You had me fooled for a second. But seriously, do I say yes to Miss Gautier?"

"Can she afford our fees, Kitty? I know you'd investigate for next to nothing, but as your *partner*—"

Clever of her to emphasize that word.

"—I insist we make the same arrangement as we do with our other clients."

"During our discussion, I mentioned our fees. It won't be a problem."

"You believe she can afford us?"

"I do. Lord Rosewood settled funds on her."

"Really? Why would he do that?"

"That's a really good question." And one that needed an answer.

"She couldn't be managing the funds herself, though. She's only eighteen, an American, and, of course, a woman."

"Rosewood must have made a financial arrangement with someone or some firm."

"Do you think he married her?"

"She didn't mention it." But then, would she? As a young woman from another country and a different race, I wouldn't reveal such a thing, not when my brother had been accused of an aristocrat's murder.

"That could complicate things."

"Now you see why I want to investigate. The press will make mincemeat of Monique once they discover Lord Rosewood made a financial arrangement for her. We have to protect her."

Lady Emma's gaze assessed me. "Kitty, if we accept this matter, our client will be Maurice Gautier, not his sister. There might be a conflict of interest there."

"We'll deal with it when, and if, the time comes. So can we take on the case?"

"Yes. Mind you, I still have concerns."

I chose to ignore that last part. "Thank you, Lady Emma." I squeezed her hands. "You're the stoutest of friends and the best business partner I've ever had."

"Your only business partner," she reminded me with a small lilt to her lips.

"For now!" I winked at her and made my way to my office to telephone Monique Gautier with the news that we would take on her brother's case.

CHAPTER 11

ARRANGEMENTS ARE MADE

*T*HE FIRST ARRANGEMENT that needed to be made, of course, was legal representation for Maurice Gautier. I contacted Sir Frederick Stone to obtain a referral. He regretted he could not take on the case himself as he was much too busy. So, he recommended a highly reputable barrister.

Wasting no time, I telephoned the counselor and informed him I was working on behalf of Maurice Gautier and his sister Monique. I didn't need to explain the details of the murder nor Maurice's arrest as he'd read about them in the papers. He assured me he would visit the prison where Maurice was being held within twenty-four hours and offer his representation.

Client-barrister confidentiality being what it was, I couldn't obtain any information from him. I would need to conduct the investigation on my own. But then, I didn't expect otherwise. My first enquiry would be with Lord

Salverton, the one person of my acquaintance familiar with Lord Rosewood.

I hadn't seen him since Gennaro's so I had no way of knowing if he was still in London or . . . somewhere else. Although I had no confirmation, I suspected he worked for a branch of the Secret Intelligence Service. In what capacity, I had no idea. But his travels abroad, ostensibly in search of rare postal stamps, told me he must have something to do with foreign information gathering.

Hollingsworth would most likely have known if he was in the city. Unfortunately, he'd gone off to Bristol where his ship was being fitted with new steam engines. But no matter. Robert would surely know. He may not be a close acquaintance of Salverton, but he worked for Scotland Yard. He'd be able to provide me with the information I needed.

"Salverton?" he asked once I'd made the purpose of my telephone call known.

"He recognized Lord Rosewood at Gennaro's. I assume he was familiar with him."

"Whereas I wouldn't be."

I detected a strange note in his voice. Did he resent my reaching out to Salverton, or was it something else? "You don't mind, do you?"

"No. Of course not. It's just . . ."

"Yes?"

"Salverton might not be able to share information about Rosewood."

Heavens! Had Rosewood also worked with foreign intelligence? "Well, I won't know unless I ask. And right now I'm more interested in Lord Rosewood's background, family history and such, than anything else."

"I see. I'll ask the sergeant on duty to look up Salverton's details. I'll call you as soon as I hear back from him."

Fifteen minutes later, Robert telephoned with Salverton's address and telephone number.

Salverton lived in Belgravia, 10 Chester Street to be exact. Unfortunately, he was not at home, but his secretary, Sidney Collier, was. That conversation proved to be quite illuminating.

"Lord Salverton is at his gentlemen's club. I expect him back this afternoon."

"Oh." That was rather disappointing. *This afternoon* could mean anything between two and six.

"Is the matter of some urgency?"

"Yes, I'm afraid it is."

"Is this regarding the unfortunate incident at Gennaro's?"

He was awfully well informed, but then he was Lord Salverton's private secretary. "Yes. I've been retained to investigate Lord Rosewood's unnatural demise. I need to find out as much information as I can about his background. Lord Salverton seemed to be familiar with him."

"I understand. Unless it's an emergency, a telephone call to his club is not permitted. But I can send round a note."

"That would be wonderful. Thank you, Mister Collier."

"You're welcome, Miss Worthington."

It was past one, and my stomach was strongly reminding me it was time to be fed. I didn't dare leave lest I miss Salverton's phone call. So I asked Betsy to pick up a Ploughman's lunch from the local pub. I'd just finished the delicious ham and cheese sandwich and crisps when Salverton called.

"Miss Worthington, my personal secretary informs me you wish to discuss something with me."

I was struck with the formal tone to his speech. But if that's the way he wished to proceed, I could do the same. "Yes, Lord Rosewood."

"Ahh," there was a pause at his end. "I'll be free in an hour or so. Can you come to my domicile? Say at three? We'll be able to discuss things freely there."

"Yes, of course. Thank you, Lord Salverton."

Meeting a gentleman at his private abode was definitely not acceptable for a young lady to do. In the past, I would have taken Betsy with me. She'd often accompanied me on sojourns to Scotland Yard and to interviews with prospective witnesses. But I was now a lady detective and a professional so there'd be no need. Still, I did not wish for tongues to wag. So I decided to wear my widow's weeds, a disguise I kept in the office. As the dark veil would hide my features, no one would be able to guess who I was.

I reached Lord Salverton's residence ten minutes before the appointed time. He hadn't yet arrived, but I was expected. Not only did Mister Collier greet me, but he had tea served in the drawing room. With its cream walls, brown leather sofa and occasional club chairs, it very much declared itself a gentleman's domain.

I'd just nibbled into a biscuit when I heard a door open and close in the distance. Within a few minutes, Lord Salverton was there, imposing in his height and breadth, immaculately attired in a navy blue, three-piece suit.

"Miss Worthington. My apologies for keeping you waiting."

"Not at all. I was early."

"You've had your tea, I see," he said pointing to the service.

"An excellent Oolong. Would you like me to pour you a cup?"

"No. Thank you. I've just enjoyed a luncheon. Now what would you like to know about Lord Rosewood?"

"His background. Family and such."

Relaxing into one of the brown leather chairs, he took up the narrative. "He studied at Eton and Oxford. Inherited his title at an early age. His father fell from a horse breaking his neck."

"How very unfortunate."

"More than you would expect. They were very close."

That was unusual. Sons of the aristocracy tended to be raised apart from parents who believed children should be rarely seen and never heard. At the appropriate age, they were sent off to Eton and later on to Oxford or Cambridge. But seemingly that had not been the case with Rosewood.

"He knew his duty and married early. By the time he turned twenty-seven, his wife had provided him with a son. Unfortunately, several years later she died from a lung disease. He never remarried. There really was no need to do so. Not only did he have an heir but a younger brother as well."

Goodness, he was rushing through everything at break-neck speed. Although I appreciated what he'd shared, I'd hoped to obtain a better measure of Lord Rosewood. "How did you become acquainted with him?"

"Ahhh." He rose and started strolling about the space, no doubt to determine how much to reveal. He must have reached a decision, because he stopped and turned toward me. "Rosewood had a brilliant mind. He possessed a facility for languages, and a rare ability to understand complex issues that perplexed simpler minds." He executed a down-ward, chopping motion. "He saw right to the heart of things."

That speech hadn't answered my question. Still, it provided a valuable insight. "He would have been a great asset in certain governmental departments—say the intelligence foreign service."

He said nothing. It didn't surprise me. Robert would have clammed up as well. I would have to take another tack. "You said at Gennaro's he was a friend of the Prince of Wales."

He appeared somewhat chagrined. "I regret saying that. I'd hoped you'd forgotten about it."

"I never forget a thing, Lord Salverton. But I will not mention it to anyone else if you're worried. Others who were at our table would have overheard you, however." When he said nothing, I said, "Something seemed to concern you that night."

"Rosewood's relationship with the jazz singer."

"Monique Gautier," I offered.

"Yes."

"Why?"

When he remained silent, I prompted. "Does it have anything to do with the prince's friendship with Lord Rosewood?" He hadn't stated it specifically, but the implication had been there.

He brushed a hand across his brow. "I've already revealed more than I should. I can say no more. My apologies."

Fine. I would find another way. In the meantime, I had additional questions.

"Did Lord Rosewood have any enemies or quarrel with anyone?"

He raised an amused brow. "Other than Maurice Gautier?"

"Yes."

"Not as far as I know, but then I was not part of his inner circle."

"Did he involve himself with matters in the House of Lords?" As a marquis, Rosewood would have been entitled to participate in that august body.

"Not that I know, but again—"

"You were not part of his circle." Guessing I would get no more out of him, I thanked him and made my way out. He kindly instructed a footman to hail a cab for me. I didn't mind he asked a member of his household to do so. It was the usual thing to do. Still, I couldn't help but think he didn't want to be seen with me. Odd, seeing I was heavily veiled. Was it a precaution? Or something else? Whatever the reason, it was doubtful I would consult him again.

Salverton's reticence had hinted at one thing—a connection between Lord Rosewood and the Prince of Wales. The palace would more than likely object to any enquiries about the prince. If I asked for the usual assistance from family and friends, word was bound to get out. And that was something I couldn't afford. More than likely, there would be serious consequences for the agency and myself. I let out a heavy sigh. I would need to conduct this investigation by myself.

CHAPTER 12

AN UNWELCOME SCHEME

WHEN I RETURNED to the office, I was surprised to find Robert waiting for me.

"Did I forget you were coming?" I asked offering him my cheek to kiss. Things had been so hectic he could have very well mentioned it, and it'd slipped my mind.

"No. Something came up I wished to discuss with you."

"Oh?" His expression was so severe I became a bit alarmed. "Nothing serious, I hope."

He glanced at Betsy. "Let's discuss it in your office." Obviously, he had no wish for anyone to overhear what he was about to say.

Betsy was quick to pick up on his unspoken command. Gathering her things, she came to her feet. "I'll be on my way, then. Unless you need something else, Miss?"

"No. I'm fine. Where is everyone?" If Robert needed privacy, I needed to know where the rest of the staff was.

"Lady Emma had an appointment, Miss Jenkins has left,

and Lady Aurelia is in her quarters." The latter always let Betsy know when she retired for the day.

"Thank you, Betsy," I said.

"May I hail you a cab?" Robert asked, gentleman that he was.

"No, thank you, sir. It shouldn't be difficult for me to do so. At this time of day, there are always some around." And then with a goodbye wave and a smile, she sailed out the door. She wouldn't be out of pocket for the cost of the cab, as that was a fringe benefit I included in staff remuneration.

After stashing my coat and hat in the foyer wardrobe, I turned back to Robert. "What did you wish to discuss?"

Rather than answer, he pointed to my office. "Shall we?" s soon as we stepped inside, he closed the door firmly behind him and allowed his gaze to take in the space. "You got my roses, I see." Every Monday, he had a dozen fragrant blooms delivered. Their exquisite perfume, never mind their beauty, proof of his love for me.

"Yes, thank you. They're lovely." He was trying to sweeten me up before bringing up whatever brought him to the agency. Somehow, I didn't think it was good news. "Won't you take a seat?" I pointed to the velvet armchair, a match to my own, I kept for guests.

"I prefer to stand, if you don't mind."

"Of course not."

He brushed a hand across his brow. "This afternoon, the superintendent called me into his office. A special matter has come up that needs the full attention of a detective chief inspector."

"And he appointed you!" I grinned. "That's wonderful, Robert. But what about your other investigations?" He may no longer be in charge of the enquiry into Lord Rosewood's murder, but he had other matters to attend.

"They've been reassigned."

A concern suddenly assailed me. "This important matter. It won't take you away from London, will it?" It wouldn't be the first time he'd been seconded to another jurisdiction. The Yorkshire child kidnapping case came to mind.

"I don't think so."

"Splendid. But why the long face?" He had me truly flummoxed.

He started pacing. As my office was not large, he didn't have far to go. Four steps forward, four steps back. And then he finally stopped. "An individual will have to consent." He scrubbed his face. "I'm not so sure she will."

"She?" Who could it possibly be? He wouldn't say, that's for sure. Neither would he share the reason for the assignment. There was only one thing I could do. Offer my encouragement. "Well, darling, you won't know until you ask." I offered him my brightest smile.

"Will you? Darling? Agree?" The staccato rhythm to his words made me uneasy.

"Agree to what?"

"To me watching over you."

I trilled out a laugh. "I'm counting on it, Inspector, after we're married."

His expression did not lighten up. If anything, he grew more serious. And then finally, light dawned. "I'm your assignment?"

He faced me full on. "Yes."

"What? How? Why?" I couldn't begin to formulate a logical question.

"Your Maurice Gautier investigation. It may reveal sensitive matters that involve the Crown. The government wants to ensure they don't come to light."

I was beyond angry. I was furious. "And you agreed to do this?"

"Yes."

How could he? When we got engaged, he promised he wouldn't interfere with any of my investigations. And now he was proposing to do just that! I didn't think so. "I will brook no hampering with my enquiries, not even by you. So, my answer is no, Chief Inspector."

Leaning down, he captured my hands in his. "Catherine, I understand how you feel. If it were me, I would be upset as well. But if you turn me down, they will assign someone else. Someone who will not be as mindful of your objections as I will be."

Freeing my hands, I jumped to my feet. It was my turn to pace. I abhorred what he'd been asked to do. I hated what he was asking of me. But . . . he was right. His superintendent *would* assign someone else. And even worse, the government could shut down the agency. They'd done it once; they could do it again.

And this time, it wasn't just me who would be affected by its closure. The entire staff would. Lady Emma's entire income depended on her salary. Lady Aurelia, who'd come to us after she'd been dismissed from her lady companion duties, had no other source of funds. And then there was dear Betsy, who'd been promoted from lady's maid to receptionist. She took such great pride in that. As much as I resented the intrusion, I had to put my ego aside and do what was best for everyone involved. But first, I needed to discover exactly what it would entail. "How would you conduct your assignment?"

"Well, for starters, I would accompany you on your interviews."

I had to laugh. "Oh, Robert. People won't talk in front of a chief inspector. They'll clam up. No. That won't work."

"I'll adopt a disguise. They won't know it's me. You've done it often enough, Catherine."

He had me there. "So you'd go incognito as my what?"

"Associate. We would not have to say more than that. As soon as they saw me, they'd understand what I represent."

"A bodyguard." With his height and the breadth of his shoulders, it would be easy enough for everyone to believe it.

"Yes. There's more."

"What now?"

"You won't be able to hold councils with family and friends. Word could leak out. There's too much at stake."

"That I realized after my discussion with Salverton. I suppose you'll be reporting back to your superintendent."

He nodded. "I must submit a daily accounting no later than ten each morning."

I sighed. "We'll be talking to a number of people. Much of what they reveal will be of no particular interest to the Crown. I'd like to keep such things private."

"I'll do my level best to keep them out of the report."

"May I read it?"

"No. You'll just have to trust me."

I folded my arms across my chest. "I hate this."

"I know you do. But I can be an asset to your investigation."

Still miffed, I glanced askew at him. "How so?"

"Well. For one thing, if someone refuses to talk to you, they will receive a strongly worded letter from Scotland Yard suggesting it would be in their best interests to do so."

I propped both hands on my hips as I considered the benefit of the thing. "That's certainly an advantage I've never had before."

"And then there's the fact we will be spending more time together."

I quirked a questioning brow. "At the moment, I'm not so sure that's a good thing."

"Really?" That charming smile of his made an appearance. "I thought you'd be thrilled."

Rather than be charmed by it, I pinned him with a hard stare. "I want to make one thing clear, Inspector."

"Fire away."

"I manage this investigation. Not you. Not Scotland Yard. I will decide who I talk to, the places I go, the manner in which I travel."

"That's agreeable as long as you keep me informed about all of it."

"That can be arranged."

"I'll need reasonable notice, Catherine. No waiting until the last minute to telephone."

"Very well."

"And you will listen to my advice. If I believe an action might be questionable or put you in danger, I will let you know."

"Fair enough." It didn't mean I had to follow it.

"And the Crown is off limits. You may not approach or inquire about any member of the royal family. That includes their majesties and all of their offspring."

"The Prince of Wales was a friend of Lord Rosewood. Maybe he knows something."

"You will not be allowed to talk to him."

"Fine," I had not expected I would, so I had no objection to that constraint. "Is that it?"

"For now. If some other issue comes up, I will bring it up."

Narrowing my gaze at him, I landed none too gently on my chair.

He, on the other hand, took repose in his usual, elegant manner. "Now, could we discuss what Salverton said?" He retrieved a small case book and a pencil from inside his jacket. I'd first seen a similar one when he interrogated me aboard the Golden Arrow.

"I asked him about Lord Rosewood's background which you probably already know."

"Anything else?"

"No."

He tucked his case book back in his jacket without writing a single word. "What's next?"

"I'll need to interview the members of the jazz band since they were the closest to the murder scene. Miss Gautier will arrange it. I'd also like to explore the club itself, especially that storage room and the exit into the alley."

"I can help you with the latter. Shall I contact the owner?"

"Please do." I glanced at my wristwatch. It was past six. "I have to go. Mother will be wondering where I am. Would you like to join us for supper?"

"Regretfully, I'll decline. The superintendent will be anxious to hear you've agreed to our proposal."

I kept my feelings as to his last statement to myself. No sense griping about it. It was what it was. All I could do was move forward. "If at all possible, I'll arrange to interview the musicians tomorrow. How should I let you know the time and place?"

He handed me a card with a telephone number I did not recognize. "Ask the operator to connect you to this number. It's a secure line."

"Meaning?"

"The conversation can't be overheard by the operator. A police officer will take your message. He'll know how to reach me."

"Will you meet me there?"

"It would lend credence to my role as your bodyguard if we arrive together. I'll come here."

I still had plenty of questions, but I needed to go home. After I locked the agency's door, we made our way to my roadster which was parked by the kerb. I offered to drive him to Scotland Yard, but he declined. He thought it best if we were not seen together there at this time. He clutched the motorcar's door after I climbed into it. "I hope this will not come between us, Catherine."

"So do I." Unfortunately, this new situation would test us in ways I couldn't have foreseen.

CHAPTER 13

JEREMIAH BLOODSWORTH

*A*S SOON AS I ARRIVED at the agency the following morning, I telephoned Monique Gautier. She'd visited her brother at Brixton Prison where he was confined until his court date. Unfortunately, laws being what they were, I had to rely on her to ask questions of him. She'd not only done so but added more of her own.

As she spoke, I jotted his answers on the journal I'd started on the Lord Rosewood murder. As a matter of course, I kept one for every one of my investigations. His responses drew a picture of his movements the night of the murder. Of course, his account would need to be verified. Something I intended to do by talking to the other members of the jazz band and exploring the club.

Since I needed to talk to the band members, I asked her to arrange a time and place for me to do so. They would be practicing at Gennaro's this afternoon, so she suggested three o'clock. If that presented a problem, she would call back to let me know. Hopefully, that appointment would prove satisfactory, as it would give me sufficient time to conduct interviews before I explored the backstage area of the club. After our conversation ended, I telephoned the number Robert had given me and relayed the information. And then I went on with my day.

Busy as I was with agency matters and a minor investigation, the rest of the morning flew by. With no time to visit a local eatery, I ordered a luncheon and barely registered the meal delivered by our local pub.

So, it was a total surprise when Betsy knocked on my door at two o'clock. "There's a gentleman out here to see you, Miss. A Mister Jeremiah Bloodsworth. Chief Inspector Crawford Sinclair sent him." Her face held more than a smidgen of curiosity.

"Oh, yes. I should have told you I was expecting him." Although I'd had no idea what time he'd show up. For the near future, he was bound to be a fixture around the agency, so I needed to account for his presence to avert suspicion.

I proceeded to our reception area to greet him. "Good heavens!" I couldn't help but exclaim.

The man who stood before me was at least six inches broader and two stone heavier than Robert. His dark unruly mane appeared not to have seen a barber's shears in quite some time. Neither had his face been touched by a razor as he was sporting a bushy beard. An ugly scar marked the corner of his right eye giving him a quite ominous look. His black suit, although clean, had seen better days and in no way resembled the bespoke ones Robert usually wore. For a finishing touch, a flat cap topped his head, rather than the elegant fedoras Robert preferred.

"Miss Worthington?" The raspy voice matched the threatening aspect of him.

"Yes. Would you care to step into my office, Mister Bloodsworth? We can talk there."

He nodded silently before coming along in my wake.

Once inside my office, I shut the door and leaned back against it. "I would have never recognized you. I still don't. How did you manage it?"

"My valet. He worked as a dresser and makeup artist for a theatre production company."

"However did he come to work for you?"

"Someone framed him for a particularly nasty murder. I proved his innocence. Recognizing his quite unique talents, I offered him a position in my household which he eagerly accepted. After the ordeal he went through, he was done with the theatre world."

"I'll have to meet this paragon."

A crooked smile barely made it past his beard and mustache. "You already have."

He had to have been one of the staff members I thanked in Robert's kitchen Sunday before last, a lifetime ago. But there was no sense wondering about it. Not when we had so much to do. I pointed to the chair Robert occupied the day before. "Why don't you take a seat? I'll catch you up on what Miss Gautier said."

It didn't take long. Thirty minutes later, we were making our way across town. London traffic being what it was, we'd deemed it best to hail a taxicab, rather than drive to Gennaro's in my roadster.

As the club was scheduled to reopen tonight, it needed to appear like nothing untoward had happened. A mammoth job. But somehow they had put the space to rights. Tables and chairs were arranged once more around the perimeter of the ballroom. Small flower vases and candles were neatly arranged. Most importantly, the renown vines were fixed once more securely to the walls. I couldn't help but notice that fully illuminated the club had lost most of its charm. The venue definitely showed best in the muted light we'd enjoyed several nights ago.

Still, I had to compliment the owner. "What a gorgeous job you've done, Mister Gennaro. The ballroom is once more magnificent."

"Thank you, Miss Worthington. The staff worked very hard to make it presentable. Although I must admit, there are still a few things that need to be repaired."

"Isn't there always? I imagine you'll get them fixed in no time."

"You're very kind." He nodded. "The members of the jazz band are waiting for you backstage. Shall I escort you there?"

"Thank you."

"Anytime. We hope to see you again under more pleasant circumstances. I can promise you the best table to you and, er, ..." He cast a dubious eye toward Robert.

I smiled. "Oh, how remiss of me not to introduce you. This is Jeremiah Bloodsworth, my . . . associate."

"Yes, of course." He cleared his throat. "This way."

The jazz club musicians were lounging around the green room in various poses and attitudes. Some were practicing on their instruments, others were smoking, and one was pouring a drink from a whiskey bottle.

"Gentlemen," Mister Gennaro said. "This is Miss Worthington. I understand she has arranged to talk to each of you about the recent sad event."

All seven members of the band gazed at me out of suspicious eyes. Clearly, this would not be easy.

I offered my brightest smile. "I'm looking forward to it."

"Who's the cat?" One of the smokers pointed his cigarette toward Robert.

"My associate, Jeremiah Bloodsworth."

"Uh-huh. I'm not talking to you with him around."

Just as I feared. Disguise or no disguise, witnesses would not open up in his presence. "We will be holding our conversation in Miss Gautier's private room." I'd already arranged it with her. "Mister Bloodsworth will not be present."

Robert cleared his throat. "I don't think that would be wise, Miss Worthington."

I waved away his objection. "Don't be silly, Mister Bloodsworth. I'm sure nothing untoward will happen."

Taking a long pull from his cigarette, the one who objected somehow managed to smirk.

"Well, I shall leave you to it, then," Mister Gennaro said as he swiftly quit the room.

After removing my outer garment and hat and passing them to Robert, I retrieved my notebook and a pencil from my handbag so I could jot down what they said. "Now, you already know my name"—I smiled—"but I don't know any of yours. If you gentlemen could introduce yourselves, I would greatly appreciate it. Oh, and please tell me what instrument you play."

"Samuel 'King' Tibideaux. I'm the band leader. I play the cornet."

I stuck out my hand. "Nice to meet you. Shall I call you Mister Tibideaux or would you prefer something else?"

"King will do."

"Splendid." I jotted it in my notebook. "You don't mind, do you, if I make some notes. It helps me to remember."

"No." He was a non-smiling sort.

I gazed at the brash young man who kept fiddling his fingers. "And you, Sir?"

"Izzy Bonom. I play the drums." He mimicked striking a drum.

Cigarette man objected. "Tell the lady the truth." Gazing at me, he said, "His real name is Isidore."

"Nice to meet you, Izzy." I made a point of referring to him by his preferred moniker.

"Now don't you go and cross him, Miss Worthington," cigarette man said. "His grand-mère is a Voodoo priestess. She can put a spell on you."

"How very interesting. I'd love to learn more about it."

"Of course," Izzy said before darting an evil eye toward cigarette man.

A very handsome young man came to his feet and approached me holding out his hand. "Jubal Johnson. I play the bass."

"Oh, I heard your solo the other night. It was magnificent."

"Thank you," he said, ducking his head.

Why, he was shy! I wrote both his name and his personality trait in my notebook. I nodded to a musician who was nattily dressed in a three-piece suit with a pocket handkerchief. "And you, Sir?"

"Baptiste Dupin. Clarinet. Enchanted, mademoiselle." When he shook my hand, I caught a whiff of his lavender vanilla cologne. I knew that scent— Jicky by Guerlain. French and very expensive. His easy charm and stylish apparel would attract plenty of women. But in my opinion his good looks did not match Jubal's.

Another player came forward. "Paul Jackson. Trombone."

"Pleased to meet you."

He pumped my hand with an exuberance I felt all the way to my shoulder. No doubt his arm got well exercised by his musical instrument.

Gazing at me, the one softly strumming a guitar, said. "Thibaut Turner."

"Let me guess. Guitar."

He nodded.

"It's a pleasure to meet you, Mister Turner."

"Likewise."

"And you, sir?" I asked cigarette man who was downing a second drink.

"Augustine Baudet. I go by August."

"How very nice to meet you, August. And what instrument do you play?"

"The piano. I like to tickle the keys, as well as other beautiful things." In the next instance, he'd not only kissed my hand, but stroked one of my fingers.

The ire pulsing from Robert became downright palpable. I needed to defuse the situation before Mister Baudet found himself in an unfortunate condition.

"Let's step into Miss Gautier's dressing room, shall we, Mister Baudet?"

"Miss Worthington," Robert said. "I must insist on accompanying you."

"Suggestion noted, but declined."

Lids lowered, jaw clenched, he stepped toward August Baudet. "If you lay one finger, or another part of your anatomy, on Miss Worthington, you will regret it." And then clutching his fist, he cracked every one of his knuckles.

Goodness! Who knew he had that much aggression in him? I cleared my throat. "Shall we, Mister Baudet?"

Keeping a wary eye on Robert, he nodded before following me into the dressing room.

CHAPTER 14

THE RHYTHM KINGS JAZZ BAND

*A*FTER WASTING A HALF HOUR with the preliminaries, I only had ninety minutes to talk to the band members. Hardly enough time, but it would have to do.

"That man of yours needs a leash." August Baudet said, straightening his tie.

"He's not my man. He's my associate."

"Sure thing." He did not appear convinced.

I pointed to one of the chairs in the room. "Could you please take a seat?" After he dropped into it, I eased into the one next to the vanity table. "As I'm sure you know, I'm here because Miss Gautier asked me to investigate Lord Rosewood's murder."

"The cops arrested Maurice. They think he did it."

"Well, I'd like to find out if that's the truth." I glanced at my watch. "We don't have much time so I would appreciate straight answers."

He crossed his arms across his chest, stretched his legs, and crossed them at the ankles. "Whatever you say, lady."

"Where were you when Lord Rosewood was shot?"

"Right there where we've just been, smoking a cigarette, drinking whisky."

"And the other band members?"

"Same place."

"No one stepped out of the room? Was someone visiting the necessary?"

He scoffed, probably at the polite term. "Maybe. I wasn't exactly counting heads." He pointed his lit cigarette at me. "But one thing for sure, nobody walked out of the room with Maurice's revolver in his hand."

I jotted down his assertion. "Were you acquainted with Lord Rosewood?"

"Saw him every night in Paris. Couldn't miss him. He sat at the front every night. But did I ever talk to him? No."

"How did you feel about Monique's relationship with him?"

He shrugged. "None of my business."

"Her brother seemed to object to it."

He shook his head. "Maurice wanted to keep that girl wrapped in cotton wool. Useless if you asked me. She was too far gone."

"Did you know that Maurice kept a revolver?"

"We all did. Knew where he kept it too."

"So anybody could have stolen it."

He laughed as he sat back. "Now what do you think would happen to a Negro caught with a revolver in London? They'd toss him in jail and throw away the key. That's what. All I want is to play some jazz, get a little drunk, and have a bit of luck with the ladies. Can't do that in jail, can I?" He came to his feet. "We done?"

I had more questions but there wasn't enough time to ask them. "Yes, thank you, Mister Baudet."

After the tension laden interview, I deserved an easier one, so I asked Jubal Johnson to step into the room. But before I did that, I shot a reassuring glance toward Robert to communicate everything was fine.

If there was something I'd learned from past investigations, it was that people almost never spoke the truth. At least not entirely. Words were often offered as half-truths, deceptions, and some times downright obfuscations. I often had to winnow what was real from the lies.

So it was a surprise to find someone who actually spoke honestly. Jubal Johnson confessed he was in love with Monique.

"Oh." I did not know what else to say.

"I never told her, of course. Even a blind man could see she'd fallen for Lord Rosewood."

"Was it that obvious?"

"Oh, yes. He brought her flowers every night. A couple of weeks after they met, he invited her to a late supper. She was thrilled about all the attention he was giving her."

I asked him the same questions I asked of August as well as a few additional ones. "What happened when you heard the gunfire?"

"Someone, I think King, barricaded the door. Some ran to the gentlemen's dressing room, while others headed toward the bathroom. There's a window there. They tried to crawl through it, but it was too small."

"Which way did you go?"

"The dressing area. Couldn't have fit my bass through that window, even if I could."

In the middle of a dangerous situation, he wouldn't leave his musical instrument behind. Amazing.

The drums player was a brash young man, very sure of himself. He asserted he could make the drumsticks sing in a fascinating rhythm. I'd heard him. He was right. He confessed he liked to drink, and that's what he was doing at the time. But he confirmed what the others had said. No one left the lounge.

King admitted he'd been the one to barricade the door. As the leader of the band, it was his job to keep everyone and everything safe. And in line, he added as an afterthought. Not an easy thing to do. Some loved the bottle, others carried on with loose women, and one in particular gambled to excess. But he believed in live and let live, as long as they showed up sober and ready to play.

"What about Monique? Did you manage her as well?"

"No. I left her to her brother."

"What about his dislike of Lord Rosewood?"

"It concerned me, I have to admit. But as long as he kept it private, it was fine with me."

"He made it public on Friday. Any idea why?"

"Maurice loved his sister and couldn't abide the thought of her getting hurt."

"He thought Lord Rosewood would do so?" I asked.

"Sooner or later, yes, he would. I've led a band or two, Miss Worthington. Seen singers fall for musicians who promised them the stars and the moon. Invariably, they got left high and dry. Sometimes with a bellyful, if you get my drift. None of us wanted that for Monique."

Once I was done with King, I talked to the guitar player. Neither he nor the musician who played the trombone had anything new to add.

But Baptiste Dupin, the clarinet player, did. Given his charming personality, I would have thought of him as a ladies' man. Seemingly, I was wrong.

"I'm not in the market, you might say, Miss Worthington.

I'm a married man. My wife is back in Chicago. After this gig is done, I'm returning home."

"Is that where you're from?"

"No. I was born and raised in New Orleans. I miss it. But Chicago and New York are bigger cities. Better opportunities there."

"The night of Lord Rosewood's murder, were you all together in the lounge?"

"Yes, well except for Maurice. After his difference of opinion with his sister's friend, he was dragged away by club security."

"Do you know where he was taken or would have gone?"

"They wouldn't have wanted him inside the club. But he wouldn't have drifted far from his sister. My guess is he remained close. Maybe the back alley?"

Lucky guess, as that's what Maurice had done. Or so he claimed. "Did you see him again that night?"

"After Lord Rosewood was shot? Yeah. He was standing over the body with the revolver in his hand. We all saw him."

"Did you hear the shots?"

"Sure did. We were all in the lounge, in between sets."

"Did you investigate?"

His brow took a hike. "We know better than to run into a hail of bullets, Miss. You might get shot yourself."

"So what happened after you heard the gunfire?"

"King barricaded the door."

"What about Miss Gautier? Where was she?"

"She'd been resting in her dressing room. But as soon as she heard the shots, she ran out. She tried to open the door out of the lounge, but we stopped her. She did not need to get herself killed."

"What did you do then?"

"I fled to the men's changing room."

"What about Monique?"

"Brought her along. We weren't about to leave her behind. Not knowing what she might do."

"And you remained there until . . .?"

"Some cat knocked on the door. A tall, dark-haired cop. At least that's what he said. Inspector something or other from Scotland Yard. Had two last names."

"Inspector Crawford Sinclair."

He snapped his fingers. "That's the one. You know him?"

"He's my fiancé."

"Oh!" For the first time he looked worried.

"He's not handling the case. Somebody else is. I'm here on behalf of Monique Gautier, not Scotland Yard. Anything you say to me will remain confidential. I will only use it to advance the investigation. Do you understand?"

"Uh-huh." He seemed doubtful.

"Did you know where Maurice Gautier kept his revolver?"

"We all did. As far as I know, he's never used it."

"He had a quite public disagreement with Lord Rosewood. Do you know why?"

"He thought Lord Rosewood was taking advantage of his sister's youth and innocence. If he had his way, Maurice would not have allowed any man near her."

"Including Jubal Johnson?"

"That cat's been in love since he first set eyes on her. But Maurice warned him away, so he did."

So, Jubal Johnson hadn't been entirely honest. "It must have rankled him when she favored Lord Rosewood."

"Sure, he was upset, but not enough to kill him, if that's where you're going. Look, Miss Worthington, we were all in the lounge when the shots were fired, including Monique. None of us could have killed him. You'll have to find your murderer somewhere else."

CHAPTER 15

JAZZ CLUB EXPLORATION

*J*UST AS I FINISHED THE INTERVIEWS, Miss Gautier arrived. She appeared calm, but her eyes were bloodshot, and her voice trembled when she greeted everyone in the room.

The band musicians welcomed her with smiles, pats on the shoulder. King embraced her. "How are you holding up?" he asked.

"Fine." She wasn't. That much was clear. But she was determined to put on a brave front. Turning to me, she asked, "Were you able to conduct your interviews, Miss Worthington?"

"Yes, the gentlemen were very accommodating."

"That's good." All of a sudden, her eyes swam with tears. She retrieved a handkerchief from her handbag and dabbed her face.

"Are you sure you want to perform tonight?" King asked in a very kind tone.

She nodded. "I need to do it. It will help. It really will. I'd like to rehearse first, though."

"Of course."

King nodded to the musicians. "We'll be on stage. Join us when you're ready."

"Thank you, King."

Once we were left alone, she gazed at Robert, a question in her eyes.

"This is Mister Bloodsworth, my associate."

"How do you do, Miss Gautier. I'm sorry for your loss."

She braved a smile. "Thank you. That's very kind of you."

"Not at all."

"If you'll excuse me," she said, "I need to get ready." I doubted she planned to change to another gown. More than likely she needed a moment to repair her makeup and compose herself.

"Yes, of course."

She took two steps toward her dressing room, but then turned around. "You will keep me informed."

"I'll telephone tomorrow."

'Thank you." And then she walked into the room and softly closed the door behind her.

"Poor thing," I said. "She's devastated."

"Yes."

"With her brother in prison, she's all alone in the world. That's a heavy burden for an eighteen-year-old to bear."

Robert nodded. Not much more he could do in his disguise. "Shall we go exploring?"

"Yes, let's."

"What do you want to see first?" He asked.

"The men's dressing room, I think."

"There's nothing there. I, er, Scotland Yard removed all the pertinent evidence."

"Still, I'd like to inspect it." But he was right. The only

items left were the men's clothing, shoes, and suitcases where I imagined they stored their things. Since I had no authority to open them and search, I gave them a pass.

"The revolver that killed Lord Rosewood, has it been verified that was the actual weapon?"

"Yes."

"I imagine that will be explained at the inquest."

"There won't be one."

I scrunched my brow. "Why not?"

"The cause of death is clear. There is no need."

"The causes of death were also clear in the Duke of Wynchcombe and the Tower of London murders."

"Those were very high-profile cases. Everything had to be conducted aboveboard."

"And Lord Rosewood is not? For heaven's sake, he was a marquis."

He maintained his silence.

Someone did not want an inquest to be held. Too many questions would be asked that someone high up wanted kept secret.

"Where would you like to go next?" he inquired.

"The storage room. I want to see the layout."

The door was unlocked, so we were able to make our way into it. The reason was soon made clear. A couple of burly men, one dark-haired, the other a ginger, were rifling through some of the furniture.

"Gentlemen," Robert said in the Bloodsworth gravelly voice.

"Who the devil are you?" The dark-haired one asked.

"Best watch your language," Robert warned. "There's a lady present."

"Pardon me, Miss." Dark-haired tugged his forelock. "We've been told to watch out for strangers."

"Understandably so." I provided our names and the reason for our presence.

"And Mister Gennaro approved it?" The ginger one asked.

"He did. You may go ask him, if you doubt my word."

Dark-haired took a longer glance at Robert and shrugged. "No. That's fine." More than likely, he was in no mood to argue with an individual who looked like Robert.

"What are you doing?" I asked.

"Not enough good tables and chairs. Many were broken three nights ago."

It had been a mad dash.

"Carry on, then. We won't bother you."

Robert and I conducted our exploration in silence while the workmen rifled through the furniture trying to find whole pieces. Unfortunately, they didn't have much luck, only managing to find one unsteady table and a chair I doubted would hold anyone's weight.

"Gennaro will throw a wobbly, he will," Ginger said.

Dark-haired scratched his head. "Maybe they can be fixed."

"Gor." Ginger pointed to the chair. "Can you imagine some bloater parking his bum on that? It'll roight crack under him."

Dark-haired bellowed a harsh breath. "You're right. I'll go give Mister Gennaro the bad news."

"Better you than me, mate. I got a missus and kids to feed."

Dark-haired took objection to the remark. "Wot's that supposed to mean?"

"Nu'thn," Ginger responded.

They kept arguing, but their voices faded as they walked away.

The exploration of the storage room did not reveal anything interesting. But then the place was at such sixes and sevens, something important could be there and we wouldn't know.

"Do you think somebody hid here?" I asked Robert.

"Someone who was waiting for the right moment to strike? Yes, I do."

"But how would he know Lord Rosewood would come backstage?"

"He did it every night. After Monique's final performance, he usually made his way to the lounge. Once she changed clothes, they left together. He had his Bentley waiting outside for them."

"Where did they go?"

"Merton Park. He bought one of the new houses."

Had he really? Monique had not mentioned that. She'd only provided a telephone number. "What about the band players? Where do they reside?"

"They rent rooms in a boarding house off Piccadilly. Close to the club."

I walked to a door that seemed to lead to the outside. "This must be the exit to the alley."

"The side alley. The one to the back is down the long hallway that borders the lounge."

I thrust the door open. "Opens easily enough. Was it locked when you first saw it?"

"No."

"So somebody could have come in and gone out that way."

He nodded.

"But how would the murderer have known when to strike?"

"You hear the music coming from the stage?"

I certainly did. It was the sound of the musicians practicing.

"The murderer would have done so that night as well.

Once the band stopped playing, the musicians would have made their way to the lounge. He could have cracked open that door and seen them." He pointed to the one that faced the lounge. "He would have had a full view of anybody coming and going. When he spotted Lord Rosewood, he could have shot him without leaving the storage room. And then it would have been a quick exit through the door to the side alley."

"You said Rosewood's chauffeur was outside waiting for him and Monique. Wouldn't he have noticed?"

"He was parked close to Piccadilly. Too far away to have seen or heard anything."

"Where was Maurice Gautier?"

"He claimed he was standing in the back alley. After the club guards tossed him out, he made his way there. He was waiting for the band to be done so he could talk to his sister. He'd just cracked open the door when shots rang out. He rushed over to find Rosewood dead on the ground. The weapon looked familiar, so like a fool, he picked it up."

"And that's how you found him?"

"Yes. He was standing over Rosewood with the weapon in his hand."

"Why did he pick it up?"

"He thought it was his."

"In the process, he left his fingerprints all over it."

"It was his weapon. They would have been there already."

"Did you find other fingerprints?"

"No. Either the killer wore gloves or Maurice Gautier is the murderer."

I raised my gaze to his. "But if it wasn't him, who could it have been?"

"That's what we need to find out."

"It wasn't any of the musicians. They all swore they never left the lounge. I believe them."

He glanced at his watch. "We're running out of time. Let's make our way to the door that leads to the back alley."

With the large number of trash cans lined along the wall, the back alley wasn't exactly pristine. But at least the aroma wasn't as bad as it could have been.

"Amazing. It doesn't smell as foul as I would have thought," I said pointing to the refuse.

"Trash removal trucks sweep the area every morning and take them away. The trucks are closed body, designed to eliminate odors."

"And reduce diseases, I would imagine." The former trash removal conveyances had been open aired, encouraging all kinds of creatures to feast on the garbage.

"Just so."

Unfortunately, the alley did not reveal any secrets. So, we made our way back to the main area of the jazz club. Monique was singing that haunting tune, *The Man I Love*, with tears streaming down her face. I couldn't help but admire her; she was courage personified.

After thanking Mister Gennaro for his assistance, we made our way to Piccadilly. Since it was alive with people being dropped off at restaurants and other entertainment avenues, it was relatively easy to hail a cab.

Once we were on our way, Robert said, "Thank you for not mentioning it."

I glanced at him confused. "Mention what?"

"You warned me witnesses would not speak in front of me."

"Oh."

"You were right. I was wrong. The disguise made no difference."

"You're used to interviewing witnesses as a Scotland Yard detective. That gives you a lot of power over people who both fear and respect you. As my associate, you had no such status. So they could easily dismiss you."

What I could see of his shapely mouth beneath his beard lifted into a smile. "They didn't dismiss you. You had them eating out of the palm of your hand simply by using your charm."

"Charm doesn't always work, Insp—" I glanced toward the driver, who was listening to every word we said." Lowering my voice, I whispered, "Charm doesn't always work. Different individuals call for different methods. Empathy tends to be very effective. Other times, a businesslike approach is best. I've even been a bit forceful at times."

He curled a finger around one of my locks. "I can't imagine you ever bullying a witness."

"Not bullying, forceful. There is a difference."

With all the city traffic, it took half an hour to reach home. I'd have just enough time to bathe and dress for cocktails. "Will you join us for supper?" I asked hopefully. "You could go home and change?"

"I'll have to beg off. I have a report to write."

"Yes, of course." How could I have forgotten? "I just wish —" Suddenly I noticed the vehicle parked in front of the house. "That's Doctor Crawley's motorcar! Something's wrong!"

In the next instance, I was out of the taxicab's door and running up the steps. Robert having to pay the driver was a few steps behind.

"Carlton, what's wrong? Is it Mother?" Had her exhaustion turned into something more serious?

"Yes, Miss, she's in the drawing room."

With my heart in my throat, I rushed there to find Mother propped on one of the sofas, Father hovering over her, and Doctor Crawley feeling her ankle.

I came to a flying stop. "What happened?"

"Nothing, dear," Mother said. "Just a small faux pas, literally. My ankle turned going down the stairs."

"Mildred," Father said rather forcefully, "it was not a small thing. You fell down several steps."

"Maybe so. But I'm fine, as you can see."

The expression on Father's face did not seem to agree.

And neither did Doctor Crawley who came to his feet to give instructions to Cummings, Mother's maid. She stood next to the sofa, a worried expression on her face. "I've put a compression on the ankle to reduce the swelling. For the next couple of days, you must put ice on the sprain, and keep the ankle elevated."

"Yes, doctor."

Doctor Crawley turned back to Mother. "Under no condition, Mrs. Worthington, are you to put any pressure on your ankle. If you do, it will be damaged beyond repair."

Mother must have finally understood the seriousness of her injury, for she cautiously inquired, "How long, doctor?"

"Six weeks."

She sat up, or at least she tried to. "That's not possible! The Ladies of Benevolent Society gala is to be held in a month. I must be up and about by then."

"Mildred," Father pronounced, "you will remain in bed. I'll tie you to it, if I must."

She tossed him a defiant glance. "You wouldn't."

"Wouldn't I?" He was dead serious. "If you're still unable to walk on your own steam by the time the gala rolls around, I'll buy you the fanciest Bath chair you've ever seen. One like Queen Victoria had."

"You will do nothing of that kind!" Mother strongly objected. "I'm not in my dotage yet, sir."

Heavens! They were facing each other as combatants. Knowing nothing good would come of it, I stepped into the fray. "It won't be so bad, Mother. We'll visit every morning and evening, Won't we, ladies?" I asked Ladies Lily, Mellie and Emma who'd been sitting quietly watching the drama unfold.

"Absolutely," Ladies Lily and Mellie agreed.

"I'll keep you apprised of the gala," Lady Emma said. "And Miss Jenkins will visit twice a week."

"Three times," Mother pronounced. "And the invitations will need to be addressed by hand."

"Absolutely. You won't have to worry about a thing."

Not completely satisfied, Mother grumbled some more. And then she finally got a gander at Robert who'd quietly crept into the room. She blinked a couple of times. "And who is this gentleman?"

"Jeremiah Bloodsworth. He's assisting me with the Maurice Gautier investigation."

"Oh." She blinked some more, and then a light dawned in her eyes. She'd recognized him. Her ankle might be injured, but there was nothing wrong with her mental faculties.

CHAPTER 16

A CURIOUS LADY EMMA

*A*FTER BIDDING GOODBYE to Robert at the front door of Worthington House, I returned to the drawing room to find Mother had been assisted to her bedchamber.

The ladies, however, remained, and they were all agog with curiosity. "So, Jeremiah Bloodsworth?" Lady Mellie asked.

"Robert recommended him. As busy as we are with our agency enquiries, Mister Clapham won't be available. And your brother is in Bristol outfitting his ship. So, he can't be of help." I sighed. "I need to stop depending on him, anyhow. He's done more than enough."

"But he loves helping out with the investigations," Lady Mellie said, disappointment for her brother clear on her face.

I squeezed her hand. "I know he does. And I've been immensely grateful for his help. Indeed, we would not have resolved the Oxford matter if it weren't for him. But he has his own life to lead, his ship to outfit. I can't ask him to give up his responsibilities every time I need help."

"What are Mister Bloodsworth's qualifications?" Lady Emma asked, ever the sensible one.

"He functions as a consultant with Scotland Yard." It skirted the truth while not being a downright lie. "He'll be my main support in this investigation."

"Does that mean we won't be helping?" Lady Lily asked in a small voice.

I could see they would not be satisfied until I spelled out the truth. "More than likely, this matter will involve very sensitive information. As much as I regret it, I will not be able to discuss this case with any of you."

While hers and Lady Mellie's faces were crestfallen, Lady Emma looked relieved. "Come, ladies. You're in the middle of your debut season. A glorious one by all accounts. And then there's Margaret's fundraiser. Surely, you have more than enough on your plates." I'd have to alert Margaret as to Mother's situation. For the near future, she would need to shepherd Ladies Lily and Mellie through the season.

"Yes. But we enjoy the investigations."

"Well, how about this? If there's an opportunity for you to assist, I promise to come running. Will that do?"

"Yes, of course." She still sounded disappointed. "But, Kitty, can you depend on Mister Bloodsworth?"

"Robert trusts him, and that's enough for me." The mantel clock chimed the time.

"Goodness. Seven already," Lady Lily said.

"And cocktails." And here I hadn't had a wash.

"Not to worry, Kitty. Supper was pushed back an hour due to Mrs. Worthington's unfortunate fall."

"Well, thank heaven for that. Not Mother's injury, of course, but supper being delayed." Between the stifling

London heat and inspection of the alley behind the jazz club, I was in desperate need of a bath.

"We should go up," Lady Lily said. "Coming, Mellie?" Lady Mellie took her outstretched hand, and together they made their way from the room.

"Shall we head on up as well?" I asked Lady Emma.

"In a minute. What did the musicians have to say?"

I had to laugh. "You're just like them." I nodded in the direction Ladies Lily and Mellie had just taken.

She raised a brow. "They think it's a lark. I know better."

"None left the lounge. When they heard shots being fired, they barricaded the door with a chair."

"You believe them?"

"I do."

"Assuming Maurice Gautier was not the murderer, how did someone get their hands on his revolver?"

Propping my hands on my hips, I said, "I thought you were too busy to get involved in this matter."

"I'm not getting involved. I'm simply asking questions."

I tossed her a dubious glance. Still, I answered her question. "Apparently, it was common knowledge Mister Gautier kept a revolver in the gentlemen's dressing room. The gun case had a lock, but it could have been easily jimmied according to Robert."

"So anyone at the club could have taken it."

"Or someone who sneaked in from the outside. There's a storage space located beneath the stage. Robert found that door unlocked. Anyone could have entered that way, headed to the dressing room, and stolen the revolver. Then all he would need to do is lie in wait for Lord Rosewood to appear."

"But how would that person know Lord Rosewood would be coming backstage?"

"Apparently, he does it every night. Once the band plays

its last set, he joined Monique in her dressing room. After she changed clothes, they headed to a house he'd bought for her."

"So he not only bought a house but made a financial arrangement for her benefit. That would suggest she was more than a mistress to him."

"That argument could certainly be made."

"What about the musicians? Where do they go once they're done for the night?"

"I didn't ask. It would have gone beyond the scope of the investigation."

Lady Emma hitched a brow. "I'm not sure about that, Kitty. If one of them has a gambling problem or a taste for ladies of the night, he might be in need of some funds and willing to provide information in exchange for some cash."

"Mister Bloodsworth will be looking into their activities as well as their backgrounds. Their London movements should be easy to discover. After all, he has the authority of Scotland Yard behind him. But I fear we may not get answers from the states as quickly as we wish. He does have contacts in the Federal Bureau of Investigation, though. So, there's some hope."

"What about Lord Rosewood's friends and acquaintances?"

"He has a younger brother. I'll try to arrange an interview for tomorrow, if not the next day." With Maurice Gautier formally charged with the crime, time was of the essence.

"Umm, Salverton mentioned Lord Rosewood enjoyed a friendship with the Prince of Wales. Maybe that's something you could explore?"

"Yes, well, I won't be granted access to His Royal Highness."

"You've been warned off?"

"In a manner of speaking."

"Thus, the need for Jeremiah Bloodsworth. Is he your keeper by way of Scotland Yard?"

"We've come to an arrangement. And that's all I'll say about the matter."

Just then the mantel clock chimed the quarter past hour, prompting Lady Emma to stand. "Better head on up. We don't want to miss cocktails. Will your fiancé be returning for supper?"

"Returning?" I asked.

A grin imbued with humor popped up on her lips. "Come, Kitty. As if your inspector would assign someone as dashing as Jeremiah Bloodsworth to partner with you."

"Dashing? The man has a scar, a beard, and hair that hasn't seen a pair of shears in at least a month."

"All of which make for a very attractive package."

When I looked in horror at her, she said, "Oh, no. Not me. I have enough on my plate with Marlowe. Now, Lady Mellie is another matter altogether. You saw how eager she was to obtain information about him."

If that were true, that would be a problem to deal with on another day. "You're awfully perceptive."

She threaded her arm through mine as we made our way out of the drawing room. "And I have a prodigious working intellect. You've said so yourself."

I laughed. "I don't recall using the word prodigious."

"It must have slipped your mind, a consequence of old age."

I stopped in my tracks at the bottom of the staircase. "Old age? I'm twenty-one."

"Twenty-two. See? You've just proved my point."

Thoroughly in charity with another, we made our way up the steps and parted ways at my bedroom where Grace was waiting for me.

~

MOTHER, of course, did not join us for supper. For the time being, she would remain in her room with Cummings, her lady's maid, cosseting her. Thankfully tonight was only family and the three ladies who resided with us.

Ned, worried about Mother, had joined us. But once he'd assured himself there was nothing seriously wrong with her, he dedicated his time to entertaining us, especially Lady Lily who laughed at his every joke whether it merited it or not. As I wished to go over my notes and think about what to do next, I excused myself after supper and headed up to my room.

On the way, I stopped at Mother's bedchamber to check on her well-being. A frowning Cummings told me Mother was sleeping and could not be disturbed.

In the past, I would have resented her curt reply. But I knew it sprung from her love of Mother. Maybe having reached the ripe old age of twenty-two had matured me, but tonight I wanted to show my appreciation. "Thank you, Cummings, for taking such good care of her."

Her cheeks pinked up, something I'd never witnessed before. "It's no less than my lady deserves, Miss."

"Just so." As she would not have appreciated my acknowledgment of her reaction, I simply nodded and proceeded on my way.

I took a seat at my desk to go over my case notes. Clearly, the jazz band members were telling the truth. None of them had shot Lord Rosewood. That didn't mean one of them hadn't played a role. Maybe Scotland Yard or the Federal Bureau of Investigation in the states would discover something about one of the musicians. But my gut told me none was responsible. They'd had nothing to do with Lord Rosewood's death.

The murderer I felt was one closer to home. The problem became finding out which part of Lord Rosewood's life had driven an individual to murder the aristocrat. Lord Rosewood was a public figure, but he also had a private life. It made sense that his brother would be the one to talk to. Seeing how I knew next to nothing about him, I would need to depend once more on a male member of the aristocracy to arrange for an interview.

Sebastian would have been the logical choice. After all, he was a duke. I doubted the younger brother of a marquis would turn down a request that came from him. Unfortunately, he was at Wynchcombe Castle and not expected back for another ten days. So, he was not available. Neither was Hollingsworth who was away at Bristol. That only left, heaven help me, Marlowe.

As enterprising as he was, he could easily make that happen. Unfortunately, he had a tendency to make jests out of everything. His behavior had caused problems during past investigations. Of course, that usually happened in the presence of Lady Emma when he was trying to get her attention. But I had no alternative. It was he or no one. I had to approach him.

But I needed to do it in a way it wouldn't alert Lady Emma. After all, I had announced I wouldn't be consulting any members of our council about the Rosewood investigation. If she found out I was seeking Marlowe's help, she would most certainly have something to say.

She tended to be a bit of a late riser, so I needed to make the arrangement early in the day. I rose before seven the next morning and headed to Father's study to telephone Marlowe. That way I would not be overheard. It was a breach of etiquette for a lady to telephone a gentleman before breakfast, or indeed do so at all. But I had no patience with the antiquated rules of the last century, especially now when I had no time to waste.

Thankfully, he was already up and about and not offended by the early intrusion. As it turned out, Marlowe was not only familiar with Rosewood but knew him well. Apparently, they'd shared an interest in finances and had been in several committees together. He agreed to meet at noon when we could enjoy a spot of lunch. He couldn't do it before as he was planning to go over his books with his man of business at ten.

Upon my arrival at Marlowe's residence, I was shown into his study where he was reviewing some documents on his desk. As always, he was attired in an elegant three-piece business suit. Together with his stylishly mussed dark auburn hair he was the very image of an aristocrat and a gentleman.

He was also a rogue, as I had good cause to know. During my debut season, he'd paid me fulsome compliments and invited me to the theatre simply because I'd been deemed the most popular debutante and he wanted to be seen with me. Another lady might have expected a proposal at the end of the season. I did not. Neither he nor I wished to marry. Of course, that had been before I'd realized I was in love with Robert, and Marlowe had developed feelings for Lady Emma.

"Miss Worthington." He came to his feet and bowed.

"Lord Marlowe." I curtsied. "Thank you for seeing me."

He flashed that roguish smile of his. "I aim to please. Luncheon will be served shortly."

"You need not have gone to so much trouble."

"Ahh, but I do. I'm famished, you see." He pointed to a delicately wrought Queen Anne chair that stood next to a round table covered with a linen cloth on which two settings had been arranged. "Won't you take a seat?"

After he joined me at the table, he asked, "Now, what exactly can I do for you?"

"I need to talk to Lord Rosewood's brother."

"And you'd like me to arrange a meeting."

"If you would, my lord."

"I'll be glad to do so. I'll telephone him later today. Shall I call when it's settled?"

"Umm. A note would be better. I would prefer not to alert other members of the household."

"I'll send a footman around then." He paused for a second. "If I may ask, why the subterfuge?"

"My hands have been tied somewhat."

"Scotland Yard or some other entity?"

"Yes."

He laughed.

Our conversation ceased when a knock sounded on the door quickly followed by two footmen carrying silver trays with plates of food which they set in front of us.

"I hope you like Yorkshire pudding," Marlowe said.

"One of my favorites," I said.

He grinned. "I believe Cook has prepared a berry tart for dessert."

For the next while, we addressed our meal. It was only after the very delicious dessert was served along with fragrant coffee that we continued our conversation.

"You were discussing who curtailed your investigation," he said.

"In truth, I don't know who issued the order. As far as I can tell, Scotland Yard is merely a conduit. I've been cautioned against conducting our usual councils."

"Because of Rosewood's ties to the Prince of Wales."

"That's my understanding."

"That's unfortunate. Our hive mind tends to come up with some novel avenues of enquiry."

I heaved a soft sigh. "I agree. So I appreciate anything you can tell me about Lord Rosewood."

"How much do you know about the Prince of Wales?"

CHAPTER 17

LORD MARLOWE EXPLAINS

"WHAT'S KNOWN BY THE PUBLIC," I said. "But I suspect given the level of secrecy surrounding Lord Rosewood's murder, there's more to it."

"And you'd be correct. Indulge me while I engage in a bit of history."

"Of course."

"In, let's see, 1910 his father ascended to the throne as George V. With everything that was happening in the realm, it was bound to be a rough transition. So he asked Rosewood for advice. It proved to be a wise decision. Rosewood helped His Royal Highness maneuver the troublesome spots until he found his footing."

"A year later, Edward was invested with the title of the Prince of Wales. As he was barely sixteen at the time, the king felt he needed a more worldly education than he'd received at the hands of his tutors. So, he asked Lord Rosewood to take him in hand."

"That was the special relationship?"

"Yes. It did not go well, though. The prince has a mind of his own. At Oxford, he resided in college rooms, dined in hall, and mixed freely with his fellow undergraduates. He played football, hunted, golfed, ran with the beagles, and drove his own motorcar. He possessed a ready wit and had a fund of good humor."

I creased my brow. "That doesn't sound like bad things."

"Ahh, but you haven't heard the rest of it. He was also petulant. If he did not get his way, he pouted. If fellow students did not rise when he entered a room, he ordered them to do so or denigrated their lack of manners. After all, he was their future king. When the Great War broke out, he wanted to enlist. They allowed him to do so. But mostly sent him on several overseas tours to keep him away from the front."

"Well, that makes total sense. The heir to the throne shouldn't be placed in harm's way."

He smirked. "Even though other father's sons were."

"That's different, and you know it, Marlowe."

"Just so. Unfortunately, after the Great War ended, he didn't moderate his behavior. Not only does he abhor protocol and ignore established conventions, but he's conducted a series of sexual liaisons that worried both his father and Prime Minister Baldwin."

"Oh, my."

"And then there was Marguerite Alibert, with whom he had an affair. She shot her husband at the Savoy. During the murder trial, the palace went to extreme measures to keep the prince's name out of the press."

"Good heavens!"

"Rosewood tried to curtail his more excessive habits, but the prince refused to be told what to do by someone he considered his inferior."

"Would he have known about Lord Rosewood's relationship with Monique Gautier?"

Marlowe nodded. "It caused a final rift between them if rumors are to be believed. You see the prince believes the white race is superior to any other. So far his prejudice has been kept under wraps. He's wildly popular with the public, and the Crown, as you can imagine, is eager to keep it that way. But innuendoes and whisperings are growing louder at Westminster."

"And because of Rosewood's connection to the Prince of Wales, my investigation may very well rake up the muck and bring it to light."

"Exactly. Tread carefully, Kitty. Whatever you do, don't let the press hear about what you're doing. They won't hesitate to blast it all over their front pages. The Crown would take drastic steps to stop that scandal from taking flight."

"Including shutting down the Ladies of Distinction Detective Agency," I said somewhat despondently.

"I fear so, yes."

"I'll try my best to keep the investigation from leaking out. But I need to talk to members of his family. What do you know about Rosewood's brother?"

"Lord Stephen. He's a vicar with the Church of England."

"He joined the church?"

"Well, you know what happens in the aristocracy. The oldest son inherits the title and the fortune, the next oldest joins the military and the third joins the church. Lord Stephen didn't feel a particular calling for the military. So he became a vicar at the parsonage under Rosewood's keeping. By all accounts, it more than suits him. He tends to be a bit of a prig."

Marlowe didn't have much more to add. So, I thanked him and took a taxi to the agency where a message from Robert awaited me.

He'd assigned one of his inspectors to investigate the activities of the members of the jazz club. But he didn't expect results of those enquiries for a couple of days. He'd also sent a telegram to his contact at the Federal Bureau of Investigation. No idea when he would hear back from him.

The rest of the afternoon, I dedicated to other agency matters. It wouldn't do to totally desert my duties. At the end of the day, I was satisfied with the job I'd done.

After bathing and dressing for supper, I headed toward the drawing room where the atmosphere was downright tense. Ladies Lily and Mellie's worried glances were bouncing between Father and Mother who was reclining on her favorite sofa. Ned, who'd potted himself on an ottoman next to her, was attempting to jolly her up. Father stood alone by the mantel, misery written all over his face. Since Lady Emma seemed to be the only one acting normal, I approached her so I could discover what drama had taken place.

She didn't disappoint.

Apparently, Mother, having grown bored with staying in bed, insisted on joining the family for supper. Father had argued against it, as he felt it best for her to remain in bed. She won that argument. With his help and Cummings, she'd carefully made her way down the staircase.

"She was smiling, Kitty, so happy that she'd managed to do so. But then Mister Worthington made a fatal mistake."

"What did he do?"

"He asked one of the footmen to bring the Bath chair he'd purchased for her."

"Oh, dear. And after she specifically said she didn't want one."

"Exactly."

"So what happened?"

"They had *words*. A surprise to be sure. I've never heard Mrs. Worthington so much as raise her voice."

"Indeed, she rarely does."

"Ladies Lily, Mellie, and I were on the verge of leaving them to it when your brother, thankfully, arrived. After one look, he took command of the situation. He separated the combatants, pulled up that ottoman, and began telling your mother the most awful jokes."

"I see. Thank you, Lady Emma." Poor Father. Poor Mother. I sighed. With Ned taking charge of Mother, I would have to do the same with Father. "If you'll excuse me."

"Of course."

Giving Mother a wide berth, I approached Father. "Good evening."

After returning the greeting, he sipped from the glass he was holding in his hand.

"How are you holding up?"

He shot me a quelling look as if he wanted to silence me, but I wasn't having it.

"May I give you a word of advice?" I asked.

"Would it stop you if I said no?"

"No." I grinned.

"Get on with it then."

"Donate the Bath chair to a home for invalids. Heaven knows there are a number of them in London. And then come home, tell Mother about it, and beg her forgiveness."

His mouth set in a stern line. "I did nothing wrong, Kitty."

"You obtained the chair against her wishes."

"I was doing what was best for her. She's exhausted from everything. She needs to rest."

"Mother spent the whole day in bed, Father. A couple of hours down here among her family and friends will do her a world of good."

He didn't appear entirely convinced. I would have to try

harder. "Can't you see what's happening? Is it so hard for you to understand?"

"What?"

"She's afraid she's growing older, less vital."

"Nonsense. Mildred would take on the devil himself if he showed up here."

"You know that, and I know that. But right now, she doesn't. She was upset enough after Doctor Crawley prescribed bed rest. And now this sprained ankle means even more of the same. Both are temporary. In no time at all, she'll retake the reins of her life. But for right now, we need to be sensitive to her needs."

"I only wanted to help." His voice softened somewhat.

"Because you love her, Father. She knows that. You just have to allow her to take the lead."

Gazing toward the floor, he inhaled a deep breath. And then he looked up at me. "Very well. I'll do as you suggest."

I kissed his cheek. "Thank you, Father."

He cupped my cheek and brushed a thumb across it. "When did you become so wise?"

I let out a laugh. "Oh, Father, the last thing I am is wise."

"I disagree." His loving gaze echoed that sentiment.

There was no time for more as just then a footman delivered a note for me. Recognizing Marlowe's spidery handwriting, I stepped outside the room to read it. By sheer confidence, Robert arrived as I did. Just as well, for I had news for him.

But I couldn't very well share them out in the open, so I drew him to the library where we could hold a private conversation. "I visited Marlowe earlier today and asked him to arrange a meeting with Lord Stephen, Rosewood's brother. I just got his note. Marlowe set it up for tomorrow at two." I gazed up to find Robert's frowning countenance.

"We agreed not to contact any of the council members."

"I agreed not to hold a council."

He lowered his brow. "You're splitting hairs, Catherine."

"I can't conduct this investigation blindly, Robert. I had to find out why the palace is so concerned. I didn't share anything with him. On the contrary, he shared with me. And he knows plenty. I got quite an earful about the prince—his affairs, his racial prejudices, his disregard for protocol. No wonder the palace is afraid of what may emerge. The press would have a field day."

A muscle ticked in his jaw. Clearly, he did not approve of my actions. I had told him I would conduct the investigation as I saw fit. Still, I did not wish to put any distance between us, so I held out an olive branch.

"Will you accompany me to Rosewood House?"

"Of course. We did agree I'd accompany you to your interviews."

On our way back to the drawing room, I told him about the disagreement between my parents and asked him to spend time with Father. There was only so much a daughter could do. He nodded silently and did as I asked. But at the end of the evening, I felt a certain chill. Had I damaged our relationship in the pursuit of the truth?

CHAPTER 18

LORD ROSEWOOD'S BROTHER

*T*HE FOLLOWING MORNING, Robert arrived at the Ladies of Distinction Detective Agency in his Jeremiah Bloodsworth disguise. As he had a taxicab waiting to take us to Rosewood House, I wasted no time climbing in it along with him.

His demeanor was his usual—affable, loving, polite. So I breathed an easy sigh. Last night's disagreement had been, if not forgotten, resolved in his mind.

Rosewood House, held by the family for generations as I'd learned from Mother, was palatial in its opulence. Almost all the gilded furnishings, in the style of King Louis XIV and the magnificent Versailles, were embellished with shining gold leaf. It was obvious the family were lovers of art. Not only did glorious paintings adorn the walls, but museum-worthy sculptures dotted the hallway that led to the drawing room.

Robert and I followed the elegant butler who, attired in a

rose and gold livery, was almost as magnificent as his surroundings. Once we reached the drawing room, he announced our presence and closed the door behind us after we entered. The chamber, furnished with an array of splendid sofas, settees, chairs, and tables, all gilded with gold and upholstered in various shades of velvet, took my breath away.

Until I noticed the gentleman standing in its center.

"Miss Worthington. Welcome to Rosewood House. I'm Lord Stephen," he said, totally ignoring Robert. He stood ramrod straight, a disapproving expression on his face. Dressed in a black cassock and clerical collar, he could not have made a starker contrast to the magnificence of his surroundings. But then maybe that was the point.

"Thank you for seeing me, Lord Stephen. I know this is a time of great sorrow. I offer my deepest condolences."

His nod simultaneously managed to convey arrogance and superiority. Rare traits for a man of the cloth. I couldn't imagine his congregation favoring such an attitude. Still, if I wanted his cooperation, I needed to show some approbation. If not of him, of the residence.

"That's a glorious Titian, Lord Stephen." I nodded toward my right where a painting depicted a nude woman reclining on a chaise lounge while her fully-clothed lover gazed fondly at her.

"My brother as well as our ancestors were avid art collectors. I prefer paintings where the subjects assume a more modest way of dress."

It stood to reason. He was a cleric after all.

He pointed to a delicate chair, upholstered in rose velvet. "Won't you take a seat?" He didn't offer one to Robert. Was the man blind or simply ill-mannered? I couldn't say anything, though, as it would be rude.

He waited until I sat before he did so himself. "I confess

I'm quite confused about your visit," he said with a sniff. "Lord Marlowe said you're investigating my brother's murder. I thought the man responsible for his death had been arrested."

"Yes. But his sister—"

He stiffened at her mention.

"—Miss Gautier believes he's innocent."

His lip curled with derision. "Well, she would, wouldn't she?" And then he finally cast his gaze at Robert, a suspicious one. "And this gentleman. What is his role in this?"

"Jeremiah Bloodsworth, my associate. He came highly recommended by Scotland Yard." That was true, wasn't it? And it comported with the tale we'd disseminated. I flashed Lord Stephen a smile. "He can wait outside if you wish."

"No," he waved a dismissive hand. "He can stay." Lord Stephen may have given permission for Robert to remain, but he did not offer him a seat. Rather rude, if you asked me. But then it seemed part and parcel of the gentleman. Apparently, he needed fortification for he approached a sideboard where bottles filled with amber liquids stood like proper soldiers and poured himself a drink. After taking a sip, he asked, "What do you want to know?"

"I'd like to learn more about Lord Rosewood. His friendships, his acquaintances, any activities that would have upset someone, that type of thing."

His lip curled as before. A signature move, and one he must practice regularly in front of his mirror. It was that good.

"My brother was a law all to himself, Miss Worthington. He did what he pleased, how he pleased, and damn the consequences. His relationship with Miss Gautier a prime example. He didn't care how it reflected on the Rosewood legacy."

Rather than react to his vitriol, I retrieved the notebook I was keeping for the case. "You don't mind if I take notes. It helps me remember."

He waved a hand which I took as approval.

"Did your brother have any enemies?"

"Not that I know of, but then the man was a cypher. I only discovered something if it became public, or if he chose to tell me." He let out a bitter laugh. "The latter never happened. He didn't trust me." He turned an angry gaze toward me. "Can you imagine? I'm a vicar. People tell me all kinds of things. Theft, envy, adultery. I tell you, the English countryside is full of sinners."

Rosewood was wise not to confide in his brother. If Lord Stephen was that cavalier about the peccadilloes of his congregation, sooner or later, he would have told someone about Rosewood's.

"Did he disagree strongly with anyone?"

"Well, the prince wasn't too happy about his liaison with the chanteuse, I'll tell you that."

"Really? How did you find out?"

"He sent George a note ending their connection. My brother left it on his desk. I, er, accidentally read it."

I was willing to wager it hadn't been an accident. Lord Stephen had more than likely pried.

"And how did your brother react?"

"With his usual sangfroid."

"Meaning?"

"He said nothing; revealed nothing. And then he left for the jazz club to see that . . . woman." He spit out that last word.

I had more questions, but we were interrupted by a youth of about fifteen years of age who arrived leaning on crutches, a matron dressed in a white uniform and white cap trailing him. The new Lord Rosewood. His strong resemblance to his father told me so.

I came to my feet and curtsied. "My lord."

He responded with a sweet smile. "Please don't. There's no need."

"There's every need," Lord Stephen said. "You're the marquis now, boy."

The youth's eyes filled with tears.

"What are you doing out of bed?" Lord Stephen barked out with a disapproving frown. "The physician advised you to stay off your feet."

"I'm tired of my room. I wish to breathe fresh air."

"Such as it is. It's stifling in here."

Seemingly, Lord Stephen was not eager to introduce me, so I did it myself. "I'm Miss Worthington, Lord Rosewood. I'm investigating your father's death."

"Are you, really?"

"Yes."

He tossed a glance toward Robert.

"My associate, Jeremiah Bloodsworth. Scotland Yard recommended him."

"But they already arrested someone? Do you think him innocent?"

"We're trying to get to the truth wherever that leads."

"I understand."

"If I may, milord, may I enquire how you were hurt?"

"I fell down the stairs two days ago. A silly thing, really." His face flushed. "Not sure how it happened."

"The same thing happened to my mother."

He smiled brightly. "Did it really?"

"Yes. Father obtained a Bath chair for her. She absolutely refuses to climb into it."

"I would as well."

Glad I was able to bring a smile to his face, I asked, "How long will it take to heal?"

"Four to six weeks." His gaiety fled. "I won't be able to

play cricket for a while. And my mates were counting on me. I'm a first-class bowler," he ended proudly.

Which his uncle dashed in the next breath. "You won't be going back to Eton anytime soon. You've got responsibilities here."

"Yes, of course." The young Lord Rosewood was deflated once more. "I've run out of books to read. I'd like to visit the library."

"Suit yourself," Lord Stephen waved him away.

"A pleasure meeting you, Miss Worthington. Mister Bloodsworth," the young Lord Rosewood said. And then he bowed his head and left hovered over by the matron.

I sincerely hoped young Lord Rosewood's guardian would be someone other than Lord Stephen. The way his uncle treated him was downright reprehensible. Did he resent his nephew inheriting not only the title but the vast Rosewood fortune? And for that matter had he resented his brother? He seemed not to approve of the relationship his brother had enjoyed with Monique Gautier. Was he angry enough to have done something about it? Like murder Lord Rosewood? And the young Lord Rosewood's fall. How had that happened? Could he have pushed him down the stairs? After all, if the young man had a fatal accident, Lord Stephen would inherit it all—the title, the fortune, everything. It seemed too horrible to contemplate, but it was something I would need to investigate. And the sooner the better.

CHAPTER 19

A DISCUSSION IN ROBERT'S HOME

*I*T WAS PAST FOUR by the time we left Rosewood House. As we needed to discuss what we'd just learned and plan a future strategy, we headed for the only place where we could hold a private discussion, Robert's home on Eaton Square.

In clandestine fashion, we had the cab drop us off a couple of streets away from his residence. By the time we arrived by way of the back entrance, I was dripping wet, er, perspiring with dew. May could usually be depended upon to have mild temperatures, but it had turned downright steamy. While in the open air, I hadn't noticed the effect, but once we stepped inside his home, I caught a whiff of myself. "Ugg, I reek. I should have gone home so I could bathe."

"You're welcome to do so here."

I gazed at him while I unstuck my dress from my skin. "And what am I supposed to wear afterwards? I don't have a change of clothes."

"Um," he said, his gaze skimming me. "Marion, the downstairs maid, is about your size. She'd have a spare uniform, or maybe a dress you could borrow."

I narrowed my gaze at him. "And how would you know Marion's measurements?"

His lips threatened to break into a grin. "I'm a detective, Miss Worthington. I detect."

He had me there. Still, I couldn't help but frown. "How would I go about asking her?"

"You won't have to. I'll have Hudson do so."

"Hudson?"

"My valet."

"He, the master at disguises."

"Just the one."

"I thought Mister Black was in charge of your staff." As Robert was the sole occupant of his house, he didn't employ a housekeeper. His butler managed the household, or so I thought.

"He is. But Hudson is thick as thieves with the female servants."

I stiffened. Did Robert allow his valet and the maids to engage in liaisons? If that was so, it would stop once I was mistress of this house.

Robert's grin, which hadn't deserted him, grew wider. "It's not what you're thinking."

"And how would you know what I'm thinking, sir?" I asked much affronted.

"It's written all over your face." He led me to a spot where we were not likely to be overheard. "I've been told I have the smartest turned-out female staff in Eaton Square thanks to him. You see, he's their fashion and style consultant."

"Oh!"

"I did tell you he worked as a costumer for a theatre company."

So he had. "No wonder you're always so elegantly attired."

"Shall I ask Hudson to arrange something for you?"

"Please." Not only was I perishing for a wash, but I was curious about the aforementioned Hudson.

Within minutes, the valet made an appearance. No taller than five six, he was smartly dressed in proper black and white livery, not a blond hair out of place.

"Hudson, Miss Worthington needs a change of clothes. I thought you could arrange a clean frock from one of the maids."

"And a fresh bar of soap, if possible," I said. "I'd like to enjoy a bath."

"Of course, Miss Worthington. It will be my pleasure to arrange it." He bowed and left.

Robert had requested refreshments to be served. Not tea. I couldn't have fathomed the hot beverage in this heat. Still, I was pleasantly surprised when a footman arrived with glasses of fresh lemonade. Iced, no less.

"During the summer, we have daily ice deliveries and twice weekly ones of fresh fruits and vegetables."

Our Worthington House cook did as well. Since Robert was trying to impress me with his household efficiency, I simply said, "I could get used to this."

As we were awaiting news from Hudson, there was no sense in conducting a lengthy discussion about what we'd learned at Rosewood House. So, we simply engaged in casual conversation until his valet returned. "Your bath awaits you, Miss Worthington. Marion, the downstairs maid, will be attending to you. I hope that meets with your approval."

"Yes. Thank you."

Robert led me up the stairs and showed me to the bathing chamber where Marion indeed was waiting for me. After a quick introduction, he left me in her hands.

"Miss," she curtsied. "We've set out bath towels, bath salts, the soap you requested. Lavender. We also have a French shampoo and lotion."

"Thank you, Marion."

"We'll wash and dry the garments you're wearing. They'll be ready when you're ready to leave."

"They require special handling."

"Oh, not to worry, Miss. Hudson is a wonder at treating all kinds of delicate cloth."

"He won't be doing the actual washing, will he?" Last thing I wished was for a man to handle my clothes.

"We'll have the washerwoman do them."

"Thank you, Marion. It's your uniform I'll be wearing?"

"Oh, no, Miss. My finest Sunday dress. Begging your pardon, Miss." She bobbed another curtsy. "Should I wait out here" —she pointed to the bedroom I'd just walked through — "while you bathe or will you need assistance?"

"If you could unbutton me," I said turning my back to her, "I can handle the rest."

"Of course, Miss."

The bath was divine. The lavender soap was French milled and smelled like heaven. As I didn't have the means to arrange my hair, I didn't use the shampoo. As I bathed it occurred to me, I should have a change of clothes at Robert's as well as various sundry toilet items. In case the need arose once more, I would have fresh garments available to me.

Once I emerged from the bath, Marion was there to help me into the loaned dress, a lovely light blue chiffon with flutter sleeves and a silver-grey lace dropped waist.

"Oh, Miss," Marion said, stepping back to look at me. "You look a treat."

"Thank you, Marion. Your help has been immeasurable."

"Ta, Miss." She said, pinking up. "Mister Hudson charged me to tell you Lord Robert awaits you in the library."

"Thank you."

"What do you think?" I twirled to show Robert once I arrived in that room.

He kissed me on the cheek. "Lovely. As always." I wasn't the only who'd had a wash. So had he, for he was dressed once more in one of his bespoke business suits. The extra padding, beard, mustache, and scar were gone, leaving only the man I adored.

He pointed to the refreshments. "Cook prepared a fresh batch."

"Lovely," I said as he handed me a glass. I took a sip and sighed.

"Anything wrong?"

"No. Just the opposite." Suddenly embarrassed, I gazed away from him. "You're going to think me silly."

He crooked a finger and turned my chin toward him once more. "I won't."

"I was . . . concerned about living here after we married."

He said nothing but kept silent.

"Your house is lovely," I rushed to say, "but I've lived all my life at Worthington House. Except for the year away at finishing school, that is. And even then, I knew I would be returning there. This will be different. It will be my permanent residence."

"Yes, it will." His gaze showed understanding.

"I thought it wouldn't feel right. But now . . ."

He raised a brow and tilted his head.

"Your staff, they've made me so welcome. I feel like . . . it will be home."

"They think the world of you, Catherine. They're eager to have you as their mistress."

That was a surprise. "How can that be? They don't know me."

"They've kept abreast of your investigations through the

newspapers. They think you're the bee's knees." He quirked a grin. "Or so I've been told."

I smiled. "By Hudson, no doubt."

"Of course. Mister Black would never stoop to gossip." He glanced at his watch. "Now shall we discuss what we learned at Rosewood House. It's six. You'll need to return home for supper. Or your mother will wonder where you are."

"You will join us?"

"Yes."

"Wonderful."

During our discussion, we agreed Lord Stephen was not one to be trusted. The man was arrogant, full of conceit, and a bully. The way he treated his nephew was reprehensible.

"I agree," Robert said.

"I fear he may have caused his nephew's fall."

Robert lowered his brow. "That's a serious allegation, Catherine."

"I realize that, but it bears looking into. Don't you think?"

"If you feel that strongly I can return to Rosewood House in my true persona and make enquiries."

"Thank you, Robert. It would ease my mind." But I was troubled by something else as well.

As perceptive as Robert was, he picked up on it. "You have another concern, though?"

"Lord Stephen could have been involved in his brother's murder."

"I don't see how. He wasn't in London that night."

"Where was he?"

"Rosewood Castle in Surrey. That's where he lives."

"He could have traveled to London."

Robert shook his head. "He rarely does. I asked the local constabulary. Apparently, his parishioners are a devout lot. Not only do they expect him to conduct Sunday services at the Rosewood church but weddings and baptisms as well."

"So how did he find out about Miss Gautier?"

"Seemingly, it was public knowledge throughout the estate."

"Lord Stephen doesn't approve of her."

"He could have found fault with his brother keeping a mistress due to his religious leanings."

"Or maybe he objects to the color of her skin."

"Whatever the reason for his dislike, it no longer poses a problem. Lord Rosewood's death effectively ended the relationship. In the future, Miss Gautier will not be connected to the Rosewood name."

In theory. In practice, I wasn't so sure. Something told me Monique's name would remain tied to Lord Rosewood's. In which capacity, I had no clue.

CHAPTER 20

AN ALARMING EVENT

*A*S IT TURNED OUT, Gennaro's had nothing to worry about. At least when it came to its business. Just as Marlowe predicted, rather than lose clientele, the club grew in popularity. Everyone was curious about the jazz band involved in the murder of a high-ranking aristocrat. And they were especially eager to see Monique Gautier, the woman at the center of the drama.

But it was an event that happened eight nights after the murder that firmly placed the club in the annals of fame. I wasn't present, so I didn't hear about it until the next day when the morning papers, with their lurid headlines, were delivered to the drawing room.

Singer Collapses on Stage
    Friday night at Gennaro's, London's trendiest club. The place was literally in full swing when the Rhythm Kings jazz band

singer, Monique Gautier, fainted on stage in full view of the club's patrons.

"Vultures!" I exclaimed. But predictably so since newspapers thrived on scandals.

While the revelers crowded around, the semi-conscious chanteuse was escorted backstage. After a short intermission, the Rhythm Kings returned to the stage without their songbird. The club's patrons were assured she'd recovered from her collapse and was sent home to recuperate.

"They have no idea what she's going through." Snapping close the newspaper, I came to my feet. "I must visit her to make sure she's well."

"Where does she live?" Father asked. After Saturday breakfast, he usually disappeared into his study. But today he'd decided to join us. Probably taking Mother's place, as she'd remained in her room, resting.

"Merton Park."

He frowned. "That's a rather new neighborhood. More than likely the roads are not what they should be. Take Neville, he'll know how to navigate them."

"Thank you, Father." I kissed him on the cheek and raced off. I needed to change into my professional attire. The casual dress I was wearing would not do.

With Neville's expert driving, it took but half an hour to arrive at the house Lord Rosewood had bought for Monique. Although she was up and about, she did not look well. In just a few days she appeared to have lost weight. How on earth could that be?

"I heard what happened last night," I said. "How are you faring?"

"She won't eat, Miss," the maid who'd opened the door stated.

"Hush, Claudine. We don't want to air our dirty laundry in front of Miss Worthington. Didn't you say you'd just baked some beignets?"

"Yes, madame."

"I'm sure Miss Worthington would like to taste them. Oh, and could you serve coffee as well?"

"Of course." Head held high, Claudine turned about and headed for presumably the kitchen.

"Please excuse her familiarity. She still treats me like a little girl."

"She's been with you that long?"

Monique nodded. "She served my grandmother. When mémère passed away, she transferred her loyalty to me. I truly don't know what I would have done without her." Her face crumbled. "Especially now."

Before I could offer a word of comfort, Claudine returned with the heavenly-smelling beignets and coffee service for two.

She took her time plating the pastries and pouring the java for both of us. A maneuver that provided Monique the time she needed to regain her composure.

After I took a sip of the sinfully delicious brew, Monique asked, "It's not too strong?"

"Oh, no." I reassured her. "I prefer a robust cup of coffee." And what Claudine had served most certainly qualified as that.

We were discussing whether Monique would return to the club tonight when a knock sounded on the front door. To my surprise, it was Robert. Since he wasn't officially assigned to the investigation, something else had brought him here. From his somber expression, I feared the worst. As it turned out, I was right.

"Anything wrong?" I asked.

"Afraid so." Facing Monique, he said, "Miss Gautier, I'm sorry to tell you, your brother was assaulted in Brixton prison."

Monique shuddered once before collapsing into the seat. Poor thing had fainted.

I called out Claudine's name as I rushed to Monique's side. To my horror, she was cold to the touch.

A breathless Claudine charged into the room One look at her mistress and she wailed.

But there was no time for that nonsense. "Can you bring a blanket? We need to warm her. And some smelling salts if you have them.

"Yes, Miss."

While Claudine ran to do my bidding, I turned to Robert, "Is it serious?"

He nodded. "He was taken to King's Hospital. They are performing surgery on him. I'm afraid it's touch and go at the moment."

Claudine rushed in with a colorful quilt and a vial of smelling salts. While she wrapped her mistress in the blanket, I applied the hartshorn. The effect was instantaneous. Monique regained consciousness in a flash.

With Claudine keeping the covering tightly wrapped around her mistress, Monique came to her not-quite steady feet. "I must go to him."

Robert and I shared a concerned look. She might faint once more on the way to the hospital. But if her brother was at death's door, she needed to see him. I nodded, a clear message to Robert.

"Yes, of course," he said. "I have a police car waiting outside. I'll take you there."

"I'll come along as well," I said to Monique.

"Thank you, Miss Worthington," she said. "I appreciate your kindness."

"You're welcome." Soon, we were on our way. As there was no longer a need for Neville, I'd sent him home.

At the hospital, we found out that Maurice had come through surgery but hadn't regained consciousness. The next twenty-four hours would decide whether he lived or died. As a precaution, Robert had posted two police officers to guard his room. No one other than Robert and the medical staff were to be allowed access.

Monique was given permission to visit him, but only for a few minutes. As she wanted to be alone with her brother, I did not accompany her but remained with Robert.

I waited only long enough for the door to close behind Monique before asking him, "What happened in that prison?"

Keeping his eye on the door, he pulled me toward a spot in the hallway where we could engage in a private discussion. "He was attacked by an inmate with a knife who managed to do quite a bit of damage before being hauled away by prison guards."

"How on earth did a prisoner have a knife in his possession?"

"It happens, Kitty. They usually fashion them out of whatever they can find."

I caught the one word that hinted at something unusual. "Usually? That didn't happen in this case?"

"No. He had an actual blade, a six-inch one. Somebody had to have slipped it to him."

"Who?"

"If I had to guess, one of the guards. Somebody wanted Maurice Gautier dead."

As we only had a few minutes before Monique's time with her brother was done, I came right to the point. "Why?"

"If he dies, Scotland Yard would not look any further into Rosewood's murder. The investigation would come to a close."

My breath hitched. "You realize what this means?"

He nodded. "Maurice Gautier did not kill Lord Rosewood."

"No. He did not." But there was something else that could be deduced from the attempt to end Maurice's life. "Someone in a position of power orchestrated this scheme. Someone wealthy enough to reach into the bowels of His Majesty's Prison and pay off a guard with a healthy bribe."

Robert did not agree with my reasoning. But neither did he deny it.

"We must find out who it is," I insisted. "When Maurice Gautier recovers—"

"If he recovers," Robert cautioned me.

"He can't be sent to the gallows for a murder he did not commit." My voice had risen, drawing the attention of a passing matron.

"Catherine. Be careful," Robert whispered.

He was right. A hospital hallway was no place to discuss my theory. One never knew who could be listening.

In any case, we were stopped from further discussion when Monique emerged from her brother's room. Worried for his safety, she wanted to stay, but it was against hospital regulations for her to do so.

But there was another problem we had to solve. Monique could not return to her house. If they'd assaulted her brother in prison, she might be in jeopardy herself. Now all I had to do was convince her.

"You can't go home, Monique. It's not safe."

"You think whoever went after my brother, will do the same with me?" It hadn't taken long for her to figure it out.

First Lord Rosewood, then Maurice, she very well could be next.

"Yes." I couldn't afford to sweeten the medicine, no matter how bitter it was.

"I'll have Claudine pack some things, and we'll move into a hotel."

"It won't be easy to find one that will provide the safety you need, Miss Gautier," Robert said. "Not on such short notice."

"So, what can I do?"

"You can come home with me," I said.

Her gaze widened. "Oh, no. I couldn't."

"Of course, you could. We have plenty of bedrooms. You can bring Claudine with you."

She argued for a few more minutes, but in the end she agreed. Rather than having a police car drive us to her home, Robert opted for a taxicab. Thankfully, a few were parked outside the hospital. It would take us to Monique's house before driving us to Worthington House.

Seemingly, Claudine had anticipated such a move for she'd already stuffed several suitcases with Monique's things.

"How did you know?" Monique asked.

An unsmiling Claudine said, "I've lived long enough to know when it's time to head out of town. Where are we going?"

"Worthington House. My home, Claudine."

Her gaze narrowed. "Is that so?"

"Yes."

"A big, fancy house, I reckon."

"Claudine!" Monique said, clearly embarrassed. "I apologize, Miss Worthington."

"Nothing to apologize for. And, Claudine, it is indeed a big, fancy house."

She crossed her arms across her chest. "Does your cook know how to make beignets?"

"No. But I'm sure she'd love to learn." That one bite I'd enjoyed had been sinfully delicious.

"Ladies," Robert reminded us, "the taxicab is waiting. We should be on our way."

"Yes, of course," I said.

While Robert and the taxicab driver were busy securing the luggage on top of the motorcar, Monique closed the door to her home. As she turned the key in the lock, a tear rolled down her face, "*Au revoir, ma cherie.*"

She wasn't saying goodbye to the house, but to George, Lord Rosewood, the man she'd so dearly loved.

CHAPTER 21

A CHANGE IN CIRCUMSTANCES

*A*FTER OUR ARRIVAL at Worthington House, I surged ahead of Robert, Monique, and Claudine to inform my family about our new guests. It would not do to simply announce they'd be staying with us.

"Kitty," Mother said as I stepped into the drawing room. She was once more propped on her favorite sofa, a blanket resting over her legs. "We were beginning to worry about you."

No wonder. I'd left around eleven and it was now past four. "I apologize, Mother. So much happened there was no time to telephone."

Everyone was there as they'd gathered for afternoon tea. A good thing for I wouldn't need to explain more than once.

"How is Miss Gautier?" Mother asked. More than likely, Father told her. And, of course, there were the newspaper accounts.

"She's fine. A little shaken, but fine. As you will soon see for yourself."

Even as I said it, the door rattled behind me. And Carlton, ever the proper butler, announced, "Miss Monique Gautier and Lord Robert."

I'd hoped to have a little bit more time, but it was what it was. "Mother, may I introduce Monique Gautier?"

"Miss Gautier, this is my mother, Mrs. Mildred Worthington."

Monique performed a graceful curtsy. "Enchantée, Madame."

No sense beating about the bush. I needed to lay out the situation as plainly and succinctly as possible. "Her brother was attacked in prison. Robert and I fear she may be next. So I invited her to stay with us."

Everyone waited with bated breath, not the least of all me, to see what Mother would say.

"Well, of course, you did, Kitty. You are most welcome at our home, Miss Gautier."

"Thank you, madame."

"I'll need to alert our housekeeper to prepare a bedchamber for you. Did you bring a maid, dear?"

My ever-practical mother saw right to the heart of what needed to be done.

"Oui," Monique responded. "She's in the foyer."

No doubt Carlton was getting an earful by now. He'd withdrawn as soon as he announced our new guest.

"Very well. Lady Lily, please ring for Mrs. Simpson." Mother turned to Monique. "Our housekeeper. Please excuse me for not rising, Miss Gautier. I had a teeny fall down the stairs and sprained my ankle."

"Oh, no, Madame. Is it serious?"

"Not at all. I expect to be dancing at a gala in a month."

She hitched up her chin. No one would be foolish enough to question that statement.

While Lady Lily rushed to do Mother's bidding, I introduced Monique to the rest of my family. "My father, Edward Worthington. My brother, Ned." They'd been sitting to the side of the room, but when we approached, they both rose to their feet.

"A pleasure, Miss Gautier," Father said.

"I had the pleasure of hearing you sing," Ned said. "You have a beautiful voice."

"Merci, Monsieur."

I conducted further introductions as we walked around the room. Robert remained with Father and Ned, no doubt to fill them in on what had occurred.

Mrs. Simpson soon arrived. After a few minutes' quiet conference with Mother, she nodded and quit the room. I had no doubt everything would be arranged faultlessly. Our housekeeper was used to sudden arrivals in our midst.

"I've asked Mrs. Simpson to prepare our Cherry Blossom bedchamber for you, Miss Gautier. It's quite lovely." Mother's most recent redecoration scheme had been influenced by her love of all things oriental. So the guest bedchambers had names that reflected their Asian influence.

"Oh, you didn't have to go through so much trouble."

"No trouble at all, dear. It's gone unused for far too long. We were just enjoying our afternoon tea. There are some rather lovely cucumber sandwiches, scones with clotted cream, as well as numerous cakes and pastries. Of course, we also have tea. Today's offering is from Ceylon. Please join us."

"Thank you, madame. You are most gracious."

"Would you like to sit with us, Miss Gautier?" Lady Lily asked.

"Of course." Monique made her way to the seating area where Ladies Lily and Mellie had settled themselves. While

Lady Lily rushed to prepare a plate for her, Lady Mellie poured her a cup of tea. More than likely, they were sweetening her up before they started pelting her with questions.

Before too long, Lady Mellie was asking if she'd been taught to sing by a master.

"I've had no special training," Monique said with a smile.

"The red gown you wore at Gennaro's was breathtaking, Miss Gautier," Lady Lily said.

"Thank you, but please call me Monique." She suddenly appeared shy. "I'm not familiar with the British modes of address. Please let me know what I should call you." Obviously, she did not want to make a mistake.

When Lady Lily remained silent, I stepped in, "Lady Lily is the granddaughter of a duke. Thus the honorific."

I placed my hand on Lady Mellie's shoulder. "And this is Lady Mellie."

"Daughter of a marquis, I'm afraid," Lady Mellie said, wrinkling her nose. "But enough about us. Tell us about your frocks. The one you're wearing today. Is it of French design?"

"Oui. It's a Chanel."

I left them to discuss clothes, a favorite topic of the young ladies. Like every other debutante, they were very fashion conscious.

A few minutes later, Mrs. Simpson returned with the news Monique's room had been made ready, and her luggage had been delivered there.

"We have supper at eight, with cocktails at seven Miss Gautier," Mother said.

"Thank you, Mrs. Worthington. But I thought maybe I should go to the club?"

Dismay clearly showed on everyone's faces, including my own no doubt.

"Surely you don't plan to perform?" I asked.

"It's what's expected of me."

"You were sent home to rest." Never mind her brother had almost been killed. And she might be next.

"I'll feel guilty if I don't sing."

"Miss Gautier, you've suffered through one event after another. You've barely enjoyed any rest. Surely you deserve time to recuperate. You can send round a note to Mister Tibideaux explaining what's happened."

"Actually, he already knows about your brother," Robert said joining us. "I sent a Scotland Yard inspector to inform him as well as Mister Gennaro."

He'd notified them so they could take precautions. Maurice had been attacked in a secured prison. A jazz club open to the public would hardly stop an assailant intent on hurting someone. Which made it even more imperative to keep Monique away from the club. At least for now.

"There you go. You can notify Mister Tibideaux that you're here with us so he won't worry about you."

"Well, you may be right. Thank you."

"Go up and rest, dear," Mother said. "The gong will sound at seven."

"Gong?" Monique asked.

"Cocktails announcement," I explained. "It's a big house."

A smile flirted with her lips. The first I'd seen all day. "How very . . . marvelous." And then, guided by our house-keeper, she strolled out of the drawing room.

Miss Gautier did not return that night or the next to the club. But she did notify King as to her new address. On Robert's advice, she asked him to keep her new location to himself.

Sunday night Robert joined us for supper. Not a surprise for he had a standing invitation from Mother. But as it turned out, he had news to report.

Rather than remain in the drawing room after supper, we took a stroll to the library. We could be private there.

153

"I heard back from my contact at the Federal Bureau of Investigation," he said. "He got in touch with the New Orleans police. As you can expect, the Rhythm Kings are very popular there. By and large, they kept out of trouble. Except for one, that is."

"Let me guess. August Baudet." The piano player who stroked my finger, provoking quite a visceral reaction from Robert.

"You got it in one."

"So, what did he do?"

"He's persona non grata in New Orleans. He cheats at cards and seduces their women. And he's suspected of stealing a valuable ring."

"They didn't charge him with theft?"

"He left town before they could serve him with the warrant. If he ever sets foot in New Orleans again, he'll find himself behind bars."

"Which means, he must stay in Europe."

"Yes." By his concerned expression, I could tell he wasn't done.

"There's more, isn't there?"

"We caught someone trying to break into Monique's house."

"Who?"

"Someone well known to Scotland Yard. Unfortunately, he's not talking."

"He'd rather go to prison than reveal who hired him?" I asked.

"Yes." He brushed two fingers across his brow. "Monique living here is a problem, Catherine." He was dead serious.

"You think someone might break into Worthington House to get to her?" Outraged didn't begin to describe how I felt.

"It's a possibility. I discussed it with your father and

offered some suggestions. He agreed with me. While Monique is living here, all windows located in unoccupied rooms will remain shut. At night, every window and door will be secured."

"Even those of the upper floors?"

"Yes."

"As warm as it is, the staff will roast."

"No, they won't. Your father was wise enough to install electric fans." He pointed to the one whirling above us.

"Anything else?"

"For the time being, you'll have a new footman on staff."

"One of your men, I suppose."

He nodded. "A bright, young constable. He actually served as a footman before he joined the force."

"Monique will still be in danger when she returns to the jazz club."

"She won't be returning. I had a word with the band leader. She'll receive a note tomorrow telling her to stay away. Given the circumstances, the club owner agreed it was for the best, although he hated to lose her. She was quite a draw for the club."

"That might work for Gennaro's, but we can't stop her from visiting her brother at the hospital, though."

"An officer has been assigned to guard her. He'll accompany her every time she leaves Worthington House."

"Is this your doing?"

"The superintendent's. After the assault on Maurice Gautier's life, he came to the same conclusions we did. That he's innocent of the murder, and someone is trying to frame him. So, the investigation into Lord Rosewood's murder is back on."

"You've been put in charge?"

"No. Bolton has."

"He's an incompetent nincompoop."

He smiled. "There's a purpose to the superintendent's madness. While Bolton conducts an open investigation, we will continue our clandestine one. That way we can operate in the shadows without alerting the villain of this piece."

"Ahhh. Does that mean Jeremiah Bloodsworth will be my constant companion?"

"Absolutely. I hope you don't mind."

"I've grown rather fond of Jeremiah." I ran my hand down his tie. "Some of the ladies think he's a handsome devil. But he doesn't have a patch on you."

"Come here."

He kissed me thoroughly and passionately. But much too soon, he brought our heated embrace to a close. "We better return before somebody wonders where we've gone."

I sighed. "In five months, we won't have to answer to anyone. We'll be able to do what we please when we please."

Cupping my face, he rubbed a thumb across my cheek, even as his gaze blazed with heat. "My darling. I'm counting the days."

CHAPTER 22

THE READING OF THE WILL

*A*FTER SUPPER MONDAY NIGHT, Monique asked if we could go somewhere and talk. The library was the best place, as it was private and we wouldn't be disturbed. So I led her there.

She told me she'd visited her brother that morning with a police officer by her side. Robert had had a quiet word with her the night before to inform her of the change of circumstances. Although concerned about the need for such security, she'd quietly agreed. But there was some happy news. Maurice had regained consciousness. Although his healing process would take some time, the physician said he was on the road to recovery.

I pressed her hands. "That's wonderful news."

"Yes. I'm very grateful," she said softly.

"Something else happened?"

She nodded. Upon her return to Worthington House, she'd found an envelope addressed to her. She handed me the letter so I could read it for myself. The letter was straightforward, so it did not take me long.

Mister Charles Morrell, Lord Rosewood's solicitor, was requesting her presence at the reading of the will. It was to be conducted at Rosewood House the following day.

"I don't understand why I've been asked to attend," she said.

"You must be mentioned in the will," I said almost absentmindedly. How did Mister Morrell know she was residing at Worthington House? "Did you tell anyone where you were staying?"

"Only King."

The solicitor probably knew about the Merton Park residence. If he'd sent the letter to that address, he would have discovered Monique was no longer there. It would make sense for him to approach King. I would need to find out if that was the case. If not, we might have a leak. But at the moment, I had to listen to Monique's concerns.

"George already settled funds on me. What else could there be?"

"You'll find out tomorrow." Normally, a will was read right after the funeral. But because she was mentioned in the document, the solicitor felt it best to wait until Tuesday when all parties who benefited could be present.

He'd further informed her Lord Rosewood's funeral had taken place at Rosewood Castle on Saturday. It had been a family affair with only Lord Stephen, William, the new young Lord Rosewood, and an uncle in attendance. Made sense. Only those related to Lord Rosewood would have attended the interment.

Predictably, she was upset. "They buried George without me. He would have hated that."

"I'm so sorry." I squeezed her hand.

She brushed away the moisture on her face and took a deep breath. "I'd like you to accompany me tomorrow."

"I'll be glad to do so."

In the next instance, her face crumbled. I gently embraced her while she gave way to her grief.

IF THERE WAS one thing I'd learned about the aristocracy, they were impressed by wealth. So in the morning, I had Neville drive us to Rosewood House in the family's Rolls Royce. Monique was dressed all in black in a stylish Chanel dress, gloves, and a fascinator chapeaux to which she'd affixed a dark veil. I'd opted for a dark navy blue, matching gloves, and a wide brimmed hat.

The Rosewood butler, of course, recognized me from my previous visit. I informed him Monique Gautier was here for the reading of the will. In a very stately fashion, he led us to the library where apparently it was to be conducted.

As soon as we stepped into the room, every head swiveled in our direction, all but one with questions in their eyes. Lord Stephen sat at the front with his nephew next to him. A gentleman with mutton chop whiskers occupied the chair to the nephew's right. An officious looking gentleman sat behind a massive oak desk carved with the rampant lions and shield I recognized as the Rosewood coat of arms. A set of documents was spread out in front of him.

There was no time for further observation as the butler was announcing us, "Miss Catherine Worthington and Miss Monique Gautier."

A very agitated Lord Stephen jumped to his feet. In outraged fashion, he pointed to Monique. "What is that jezebel doing here?"

Monique hitched a breath but somehow maintained her dignity against the insult hurled at her.

"I asked Miss Gautier to attend," the gentleman seated behind the desk explained. Had to be Mr. Morrell, the solicitor. "She's a beneficiary under Lord Rosewood's will."

Lord Stephen's head jerked toward him. "She's what?"

"All will be explained in good time," Mister Morrell answered.

The mutton-chop whiskered gentleman addressed Lord Stephen in no uncertain terms. "Sit down, Stephen. Let Mister Morrell get on with his duty."

Lord Stephen blustered some more before obeying the older gentleman's command.

Turning to us, the mutton-chop whiskered gentleman said, "I'm Heathcote, maternal uncle to George, godfather to William. My apologies, ladies, for Stephen's outburst. Please come sit." He pointed to two chairs that were located behind him and far from his nephew.

Once we'd done so, Mister Morrell cleared his throat. "Lord Rosewood visited me shortly after his return from Paris and asked me to draft a new will. The reason will soon be made clear."

"As per the law of primogeniture, his beloved son, William, will inherit the title and the entailed Rosewood properties, including Rosewood Castle in Surrey, Rosewood House in London, as well as numerous other properties located throughout England. All in all, a fortune totaling 250,000 pounds."

"I'd rather have my father back," William said, in a trembling voice.

Lord Heathcote patted his shoulder. "Good lad."

The solicitor listed various sundry legacies to the staff, including the butler and the former Lord Rosewood's valet.

"Oh, get on with it," Lord Stephen barked out.

"To my brother Stephen, I leave him all my love and the continued husbandry of the Rosewood Castle church. Furthermore, I will him a stipend of 1,000 pounds per annum to keep him in the comfort he so richly deserves."

"A thousand pounds? Is that all?"

The solicitor glanced at him over his pince-nez glasses. "Yes, sir."

"Stop complaining, Stephen," Heathcote said. "That's more than enough to keep you in comfort."

"If I may continue," Mister Morrell said.

Heathcote waved his approval.

"If my beloved son, William, is still a minor, I put him in the guardianship of Lord Heathcote until he's eighteen years of age."

Lord Stephen whirled on Heathcote. "Did you know about this?"

"Of course. Rosewood would have never assigned me as guardian to William without my consent."

"He should have chosen me."

Heathcote cleared his throat. "Given your vast ecclesiastical duties, your brother did not wish to impress upon you the responsibility of raising his son."

There was more to it than that. Lord Rosewood had to have noticed the way Lord Stephen treated his son. The last thing he would have done was put William in his brother's care.

"And now we come to the final bequest. To my beloved, Monique Gautier, I leave 50,000 pounds, the Paris apartment, and the Merton Park property, along with numerous pieces of jewelry enumerated below."

Practically frothing at the mouth, Lord Stephen jumped to his feet. "Fifty thousand pounds to a tart?"

"Lord Stephen, please," Mister Morrell cautioned.

"She's nothing but his whore."

161

Monique came to her feet. Apparently, she'd had enough. "I was no such thing, Lord Stephen. I was his wife."

"Liar!" Lord Stephen spit out. "He would have never married you."

"It's true, Lord Stephen," the solicitor said. "Lord Rosewood left the marriage certificate with me for safekeeping. They married in Paris."

"She paid you off, didn't she?" The vicar snarled at the solicitor. "She bribed you to lie."

Mister Morrell stiffened with outrage. "I beg your pardon."

Heathcote stood and grabbed Lord Stephen's arm. "That is quite enough." He dragged him to the library entrance and shoved him out the door. Having done so, he turned the lock.

Sadly, the emotional outbursts seemed to affect Monique and she collapsed on the chair. "I can't . . . breathe."

"Someone, please fetch a glass of water." I said in a rush as I curled my arm around her shoulders to keep her upright.

In but a few moments, William was there, leaning on a crutch, a cup of tea in his free hand. "It's the only thing we have on hand."

"It will do, thank you." Turning to Monique, I brought the cup to her lips. "Drink."

She took a sip and shuddered. "Thank you. It's the heat." But somehow that sip had helped as she breathed an easy sigh. "Coming from New Orleans, you'd think I'd be used to it."

"You've been away from home for a while." I deeply regretted not asking Robert to accompany us. Who would have known the reading of the will would be such a disaster?

I glanced toward Mister Morrell. "If you're done, I think it would be best if we left."

"Yes, of course," the solicitor said. "I will visit you, Lady

Rosewood, to arrange for the transfer of the properties and the funds."

"Thank you," Monique said in a faint voice. "That would be so kind."

"You sent your letter to Worthington House. How did you know where she was staying?"

"The band leader, Mister Tibideaux. He was quite reluctant to provide me with the information, I might add. But he finally did so, when I showed him my credentials."

Good to know King hadn't taken Mister Morrell's word but had demanded proof.

Lord Heathcote accompanied us to the front door, probably to make sure Monique wasn't accosted once more by Lord Stephen. Thankfully, he was nowhere in sight.

"Thank you, monsieur," Monique said. "You remind me of George. He was very kind as well."

Once we climbed into the Rolls, I asked Neville to hurry as Miss Gautier was not feeling well. We arrived at Worthington House in record time. Monique only made it as far as the drawing room before she suffered another collapse. Quite concerned, I asked Carlton to find Claudine.

She arrived in a lather. "I knew this was going to happen. It's that corset's fault. But she couldn't fit into the gown."

"Let's help her to her room. She can rest there."

With Claudine on one side of Monique and me on the other, we managed to get her up the stairs.

"Make sure she rests. If you need anything at all, please let us know."

"Something cool to drink would be nice."

"I'll have someone bring it to you."

"Thank you, Miss Worthington."

At the same time I took care of her request, I asked Grace to bring me something to eat. Having missed my luncheon, I was feeling a bit peckish. While I waited for the meal to arrive, I jotted down what transpired at the reading of the will. What occurred, what was said. No element was too small. After reading over the account, I realized I'd left out a small detail. A crucial one. I hadn't realized its import at the time. But—heaven help me—I did now. And it was something that Robert needed to know as soon as possible.

Hopefully, he would be in his office. It was only two o'clock. I headed to Father's study so I could discuss the matter without someone overhearing it. But he wasn't available. Disappointed, I left word for him to call me. He would know it was urgent. I then telephoned his home and left the same message. Now all I had to do was wait.

CHAPTER 23

A DECISION IS MADE

*B*Y THE TIME I DRESSED FOR SUPPER, I hadn't heard from Robert. Still, I held out hope he would arrive in time for cocktails. He wasn't in the drawing room when I arrived, but Sebastian and Hollingsworth were there.

After greeting everyone, I gravitated toward them. Turned out the steam engine installations on Hollingsworth's ship were proceeding smoothly. So for the moment, nothing else needed his attention. And Sebastian claimed his estate manager was so efficient his presence was more hindrance than help. So he'd returned to London to be with Margaret who was standing by his side her arm twined around his.

"I heard you're investigating Lord Rosewood's murder," Hollingsworth said. Of course, he wouldn't have known. He left before Monique had visited the detective agency.

"His sister requested my help."

"I'm back in town. For the time at least," Hollingsworth said. "Anything I can do, I'll be glad to help."

"Thank you. I'll keep that in mind," I said almost absent-mindedly. Where was Robert?

Sebastian wisely kept silent. More than likely, he'd already heard an earful from Margaret.

Marlowe and Lady Emma shared a settee on the far side of the space. But once more they appeared to be at outs with each other for she only spoke in monosyllables when he addressed her. On the other hand, Ned and Lady Lily were enjoying themselves, evidenced by their constant laughter. Lady Mellie was seated next to Mother quietly holding a conversation with her.

As I was wondering about Father, he made an appearance and headed straight toward Mother. "I have a present for you," he said, extending an exquisitely wrapped box toward her.

"Whatever for, Edward?" she asked, accepting it.

"You'll see."

Lady Mellie quietly quit the ottoman to make room for Father who wasted no time availing himself of the seat.

We all waited with bated breath for Mother to open the box. Inside was an envelope with a letter tucked inside. After reading it, her eyes swam with tears, "Oh, Edward."

He leaned over and kissed her cheek. "I sincerely apologize for upsetting you and hope this small gift compensates for any hurt I caused."

We were all dying of curiosity, but I was the only one brave enough to ask. "What does it say, Mother?"

"Your father," she squeezed his hand, "donated the Bath chair, as well as two thousand pounds, to the Home for Invalids. In my name!" Tears coursed down her cheeks.

From somewhere in the depths of his coat, Father found a handkerchief which he used to brush the moisture from her face.

I gently guided everyone to the other side of the room to give them some privacy.

Just as well for Lady Lily wasted no time asking, "How did the reading of the will go, Kitty?"

I would need to talk with Monique before I shared what occurred this morning. So, I simply said, "As well as could be expected."

"I heard she was overcome by the heat,"she said. Neither she nor Lady Mellie had been present when we arrived. With the weather as hot as it was, they'd gone to Gunter's Tea Shop for ices.

"Unfortunately. She's resting in her room at the moment. Her maid is taking very good care of her."

"That's good."

It wasn't until Carlton announced dinner that Robert made an appearance. The expression on his face did not convey good news.

"Anything wrong?"

"Later. After supper."

As soon as the meal was done, Robert and I excused ourselves and headed to the library once more.

Before I could ask why he had such a long face, he asked, "What happened at the reading of the will?"

I explained the entire sequence of events. "I don't know if we can keep this under wraps, Robert. It's bound to leak out that she and Lord Rosewood were married. And once it does, the press will make mincemeat out of her."

"Well, it'll battle front and center with what happened today at Scotland Yard."

"What do you mean?"

"The superintendent was ordered to hold a press conference announcing that the investigation into Rosewood's murder had been reopened. A mistake, in my opinion. They should have simply said Scotland Yard was looking at other avenues of enquiries."

"That's the same thing, isn't it?"

"Not if you phrase it correctly."

A light glimmered. "Reopening the investigation meant that Scotland Yard had closed it."

"Exactly. But once Maurice Gautier was assaulted in prison, it became rather obvious that he was innocent."

"So they're doing it to save face."

"There was probable cause, Catherine. But even so, it should have been investigated further. Instead, they charged him with the crime to appease those who demanded someone be held to account."

"So, what happened at the press conference?"

"What you would expect. The reporters, smelling blood on the water, began asking questions, each more outrageous than the next. No answer satisfied them. Finally, one of them flat out asked if the prince was involved. Well, that question provoked the superintendent's ire. He blared out that repugnant question did not dignify an answer."

"And he didn't have the presence of mind to shut down the press conference?"

"That would have made it worse. But that's not all."

I dreaded what he would say next.

"Your name, as well as the Ladies of Distinction Detective Agency, were mentioned."

My stomach did a somersault. "What did they say?"

"That Monique Gautier had hired you to investigate the murder. That she felt the rift between Lord Rosewood and the Prince of Wales should be examined more closely. The implication, of course, being that His Royal Highness is somehow responsible for Rosewood's death."

The meal I'd just eaten threatened to reemerge. "She never said any such thing!"

He scrubbed his face. "As most things the gossip rag reporters run with, it's half-truth, half lies. As you can imagine, it was open season after that."

"Wherever could the reporter have heard about the rift?"

"It wasn't exactly a secret, Catherine."

"We tried so hard not to tie the prince to the murder. All for naught." But there was no sense crying over spilt milk. What's done is done. Needing to think, I took to pacing the floor. After a minute, I stopped in front of Robert. "Given the cat is out of the bag—"

"No."

"Robert, be sensible. We have no leads. The situation is spinning out of control through no fault of our own. We have to convene the Investigative Committee." I glanced at my watch. Ten o'clock. "Not tonight. It's too late. Sebastian and Hollingsworth were traveling all day, and we all need to be fresh."

It took another ten minutes to talk him around, but finally, reluctantly, he agreed. We returned to the drawing room and announced we'd be convening an investigative committee to investigate Lord Rosewood's murder.

"But I thought it would not be a good idea to do so," Lady Lily said.

"Matters have changed. I can't explain. Not tonight." I paused for a moment. "I don't expect all of you will wish to participate, responsibilities being what they are. But if you are willing to do so, I would greatly appreciate your assistance. And I feel comfortable in saying so would Monique. We'll be meeting tomorrow at two, here in the library. If that's acceptable with you, Mother?"

"Of course, dear. Whatever you need."

"Thank you." I allowed my gaze to roam over every person in the room. "Please think it over."

A couple of head nods, some questions in eyes, but at least no one outright said they wouldn't attend.

Beyond exhausted, I said my good nights.

Robert accompanied me to the staircase holding my hand. "You'll be all right?"

"I expect I'll spend half the night tossing and turning in bed."

He feathered a chaste kiss on my cheek, probably because a footman stood nearby. But I needed more than that.

Wrapping my arms around him, I kissed his mouth. He wasn't slow to respond, just the opposite. Still, we couldn't give flight to our passion, not with the footman bearing witness, not when someone could emerge from the drawing room. So I ended the kiss and rested my cheek against his chest. We stood like that for a while, breathing each other in, feeling each other's heartbeat. Sooner than I wished, I let go. "I better go up."

He cupped my face. "Good night, my love."

As I made my way up the stairs, I sensed his gaze on me. I would not be the only one losing sleep tonight.

CHAPTER 24

MONIQUE'S MALADY

I WAITED UNTIL TEN O'CLOCK the following morning to visit Monique. Claudine, of course, answered my knock.

"I would like a word with Miss Gautier. Is she able to receive visitors?" I didn't want to presume she would be.

In her inimitable Louisiana accent, she said, "Well, she might not be up to passing a good time, but she'll do."

I swallowed back a grin. "That's good to know."

I found Monique seated on the white settee in the small sitting room. She was gazing out the large window into Mother's Japanese garden.

As soon as I stepped into the room, she came to her feet. "Miss Worthington."

I gestured for her to retake her seat. "No need to rise. How are you feeling?"

"Better. Thank you. I believe I'll be able to join the family for supper tonight." Dressed in a flowing dolman sleeve silky robe dress, the color of her favorite shade of red, she looked much better than the last time I'd seen her. But not as well as she'd been before.

I'd come here to ask a very particular question, but I couldn't simply blurt it out. "Are you enjoying Mother's garden?"

"Yes, it's so beautiful . . . and peaceful."

"I'm so glad you're enjoying it." Guided by Sebastian's vast knowledge of botany, Mother had designed the garden to reflect those exact qualities. It blossomed with azaleas, wisteria, and iris, as well as an ornamental cherry tree and bamboo. White lotus flowers floated in the small pond which lay at its center. Stone lanterns bordered the pond. She'd even had the staff build a small pergola where someone could quietly contemplate the pond. "You must tell Mother. She'd be ever so pleased."

"I will next time I see her. She's a very special lady."

"That she is."

"Would you like some tea?" She laughed in a self-deprecating style.

"What's so amusing?" I asked.

"I'm in your home and here I am offering tea to you."

"But this is your room, so it's the appropriate thing to do. I just had breakfast, so there's no need. But thank you for the offer." It was time to ask my question. I'd hesitated long enough. "I'd like to ask a personal question, if I may."

Her gaze did not communicate permission. Still, she nodded.

"Are you expecting a child?"

She gasped. "How did you know?"

"The fainting spells, your lack of appetite. All signs of the early months of pregnancy." My sister had covered that subject during our discussion about marital relations. Something I'd been very curious about. Margaret, being Margaret, had been very thorough. She'd particularly insisted on the need for a doctor's care. "Have you seen a physician or discussed your condition with a midwife?"

"No." She ducked her chin. "I only realized I was carrying George's child shortly before we left Paris. Here in London, I didn't know where to go."

"You should be seen by someone experienced in childbirth. Just to put your mind at ease. I'll be glad to contact our physician, Doctor Crawley. I'm sure he can suggest someone. Would you like me to do that?"

"I wouldn't have to visit their office?"

"We can ask the physician or midwife to attend to you here if you prefer." Mother had never gone to a hospital to have her babies. She'd been attended by midwives for every birth. In my opinion, it was a better way. The mortality rate of childbearing women in hospitals was atrocious.

"I would."

"Mother will have to know," I explained as kindly as I could. "Do you want me to tell her or would you like to do it yourself?"

Her hands became restless. "I wouldn't know how."

"She's a very understanding sort. Knowing her, she'll want to help in any way you wish."

She breathed out a relieved sigh. "Then, yes, please do." She drew a protective hand across her belly. "But I would prefer no one else learn about my condition."

Understandably so. Only those present at the reading of the will knew she and Lord Rosewood had married. If word got around, they would think her child illegitimate. She'd be branded in derogatory terms, such as the ones Lord Stephen had hurled at her. But there was one other person who had to be told. "Father will have to know as well."

"Of course. Secrets shouldn't be kept between husbands and wives. George and I had none."

I wasn't so sure about that. I had nothing to base that feeling on other than intuition.

"I'll let you know as soon as matters are arranged. In the meantime, is there anything you need?"

"No, thank you. Your staff has been very kind."

"That's good to know." After a quick goodbye, I took my leave. First order of business was to find Mother who should be resting in her room.

Except she wasn't.

She was in her personal parlor addressing her correspondence. "Hello, Kitty, dear."

"Hello." At least she had taken repose on a sofa and propped her leg on a cushion. Taking the advice I'd given to Father, I didn't rail at her. I didn't even ask how she was doing. She would have hated that. Instead, I voiced the reason I'd sought her out. "I hope I'm not interrupting, but there's something I'd like to discuss."

She gazed up from the lap desk that lay across her middle. "You're not, dear. I'm done. Writing letters to the more generous supporters of the Ladies Benevolent Society is very important. They appreciate the personal touch."

"I'm sure they do." I sat on the ottoman situated next to her, the same one Ned and Lady Mellie had used. "It's about Monique."

A knowing smile curved her lips. "She's expecting a child."

My jaw dropped. "How did you know?"

"Cook tells me her food trays are returned hardly touched. And then there are all those dizzy spells she's been having."

Should have known she'd figured it out. She always did. "You're a wonder, Mother."

"Yes, dear. Has she seen a medical practitioner?"

My ever-practical mother getting right to the heart of the

matter. "No. But she'd like to. I volunteered to call Doctor Crawley to obtain a reference."

"You'll need privacy. Telephone him from your father's study. In the meantime, I'll ask Cook to prepare some special meals for Miss Gautier, something guaranteed to nourish but not cause stomach upset."

"Monique doesn't wish her pregnancy to be known. Other than you and Father, that is."

"Don't worry. I'll suggest the dishes reflect Monique's cuisine back home."

I laughed. "New Orleans fare tends to be hot and spicy."

"Well, you might know that, but the staff won't." Mother pressed my hands. "Leave it to me, Kitty. Now, ring for Cook."

Having done so, I proceeded to Father's study to telephone Doctor Crawley. Thankfully, he was able to provide the name of an excellent midwife. I wasted no time calling her. She'd be glad to visit Monique the next day.

When I stopped by to inform Monique, I discovered that Mother had sent her a note congratulating Monique on the happy event to be and directing Monique to tell her if she needed anything. She also told her Cook would be preparing special dishes for her. If Monique had any suggestions, all she needed to do was ask.

I'd intentionally put off reading the morning papers until after I'd dealt with Monique's situation. Having done so, I returned to my bedroom with the morning editions.

Just as I feared, the articles were indeed alarming. With their half-truths and half lies, every report had been carefully crafted to provoke a scandal. Worse than that, my name was mentioned which meant I could no longer conduct the investigation in the shadows.

CHAPTER 25

THE INVESTIGATIVE COMMITTEE MEETS

*I*N THE END, all my worry about who would attend the meeting was for naught. Everyone was there. Robert and I, of course, Margaret and Sebastian, Lady Lily and Ned, Lady Mellie and Hollingsworth, Marlowe, and to my surprise, Lady Emma.

When I raised an enquiring brow at her, she rightfully interpreted the message and responded accordingly, "For the moment, things are somewhat slow at the agency. Nothing Lady Aurelia and Mister Clapham can't handle."

"And if something urgent comes up?"

"They know where to find us."

She did have a point. After all, we were only a telephone call away. Getting on with the meeting, I handed Margaret a notebook for her scribe duties. Not only was she an excellent note taker, but it was something the scholar in her loved to do.

Robert had arrived half an hour earlier so we could plan

how to conduct the meeting. We'd decided I would share what we'd learned and he would talk about his actions and those of Scotland Yard. Nothing confidential, of course. Only what was public knowledge.

However, before we even got started, Lady Mellie had a question. "Where's Jeremiah Bloodsworth? Shouldn't he be here as well?"

"He's otherwise occupied this afternoon," I replied.

"Oh, that's a shame. I was rather looking forward to seeing him again."

"Who's this person?" Hollingsworth asked brows drawn.

"Kitty's associate," Lady Mellie answered. "He came highly recommended by Inspector Crawford, er, Lord Robert." She huffed out a breath. "I apologize, but I find myself in a quandary as to how best to address you," she said gazing at Robert.

"Whichever way makes you comfortable," he replied.

With the change in Robert's circumstances, everyone kept stumbling over his name. Figuring it would work itself out, I'd evaded the topic, but clearly that wasn't the case. We needed to deal with the issue once and for all. "Since Robert is now Detective Chief Inspector Crawford Sinclair at Scotland Yard, why don't we address him as such?" I glanced at Robert. "If that's acceptable to you, that is."

"Whatever you think is best, Catherine."

"That's rather a mouthful, don't you think?" Lady Emma pointed out.

"How about Sinclair when he's among friends?" Marlowe suggested.

Seemingly, I'd made matters worse. "Address him whichever way you please. He's sure to answer however you do," I said somewhat frustrated. "Now, can we please get on with the reason for our being here?"

But that was not to be. Hollingsworth had a question of

177

his own. "Kitty's associate. He goes by Jeremiah Bloodsworth?"

"Just so." Robert darted a pointed glance at Hollingsworth. Whatever was conveyed in that message, it was enough to silence the marquis.

It took a full half hour to explain where the investigation stood and the conclusions we'd drawn. At the end of our recitation, as expected, there were questions.

"Could we return to the night of the murder?" Margaret asked.

"Of course." Robert replied. "What would you like to know?"

"Since neither Sebastian nor I were there when the shots were fired, could you describe what you saw, what you heard?"

"I'd be glad to. The band had taken a recess. During that time, the waiters were delivering last call cocktails. People were talking, laughing, enjoying themselves when suddenly a shot rang out."

"Just one?" Margaret asked.

"Followed by two others within a second or two. I asked Salverton if he was carrying his service weapon."

"Why would—"

I raised my hand to stop her. "I apologize, but Robert can't answer that question."

She blinked but moved on. "Very well. So what happened next?"

"Salverton and I raced toward the sound of the shots which seemed to have come from the backstage area. We only made it halfway there before we found our way blocked by the club patrons who were beginning to panic. After fighting our way through them, we finally arrived backstage. The backstage area was empty. Except for Lord Rosewood who lay on his back, arms spread out, three wounds on his chest."

I swallowed hard. I faint at the sight of the blood so I was glad I'd been spared that sight.

"Which way was he facing?"

"Here." I handed her an illustration I'd done. "I drew a sketch from Robert's description."

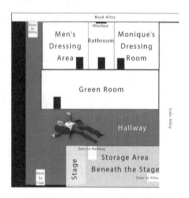

"So his head pointed to the entrance to the green room and his feet toward the storage area."

"Yes," Robert answered.

"That's why you believe someone was hiding out in the storage area beneath the stage. If somebody had shot at him from the green room, his body would be pointing the other way."

"Exactly so," Robert said.

"It could not have been any of the musicians," I said. "To a man, they swore they were all in the green room at the time the shots were fired."

"What about Maurice Gautier?" Sebastian asked.

"He was standing over the body, a revolver in his hand. His own, as it turned out," Robert said.

"No wonder you arrested him," Margaret said. "The evidence pointed toward him being the murderer."

"Except he isn't," I said. "The prison attack on his life proves his innocence."

Margaret frowned. "Why do you think that?"

As Robert was not likely to voice the reason, I answered the question. "Scotland Yard would have stopped investigating the murder if Maurice Gautier had been killed."

Robert did not agree with my statement. Neither did he disagree. So it was up to me to proffer the theory we'd discussed. "Somebody framed Maurice Gautier for Lord Rosewood's murder. That same someone more than likely arranged for a guard to hand a knife to a prisoner who would use it to kill Mister Gautier. The question now becomes who?"

"Has the guard been identified?" Hollingsworth asked.

"Not as of yet," Robert answered. "Scotland Yard is conducting an investigation."

"Only a powerful, wealthy person could have arranged such a thing," Sebastian said.

"That's my guess, as well."

While we all pondered that point, Lady Emma took a different tack. "Why was Rosewood in Paris? He remained there because of Monique Gautier, but why was he there in the first place?"

"Monique said he was attending a meeting," I replied. "He didn't say what it was, but she thought it had something to do with the British government."

"We'll need to find out," Lady Emma said. "I think it matters."

"If it has to do with the government, Salverton would know," Hollingsworth suggested.

"Unfortunately, Salverton is not talking about that facet of Lord Rosewood's life," I said. "He said he was brilliant, spoke several languages, and possessed a rare ability to understand complex issues that perplexed simpler minds."

"Sounds like a perfect description of someone who works in intelligence," Margaret said.

"Salverton might tell me," Hollingsworth suggested. He'd known Salverton since their Oxford days. So he'd be aware of the kind of information Salverton was likely to know.

"I don't think friendship will be enough in this case. But" —I glanced at Robert—"it might be if approached in another manner."

"Such as?" Robert asked.

"Scotland Yard has reopened the investigation. Today's newspapers blasted that tidbit all over their front pages. If past is prologue, they'll publish one outrageous story after another to drive up sales. Those reports will more than likely drive the public into a frenzy. And the press won't stop until Rosewood's murderer is caught."

"Sadly, all true," Lady Mellie said.

"If Rosewood was involved in some secret endeavor," I continued, "the government would not want the public to catch a whiff of it. But with every eager beaver reporter on the trail, that just might happen. You could approach Salverton and make the argument the sooner we discover Rosewood's murderer, the sooner the hue and cry will die down. He might be willing to tell us what we need to know."

"That's brilliant, Kitty," Lady Lily said.

"Not to mention downright Machiavellian," Hollingsworth said. "But he'd need to get approval from those in command, though. And those wheels grind exceedingly slowly."

Time was the one thing we didn't have. Still, we had to try. I turned to Robert. "Will you do it?"

He nodded. "As soon as we're done, I'll telephone him

requesting a meeting. He would have read the papers. Being the smart fellow he is, chances are he's already figured it out."

"All right," I said, more optimistically than I'd felt so far. "That's one avenue of investigation. Anyone else have other suggestions?"

Sebastian spoke up. "Rosewood was being considered for Lord High Chancellor. I'd go so far as to say he was the front runner. Lord Marsh's name was also tossed around. And he's made it obvious it's something he very much desires."

"Lord Marsh doesn't deserve that honor," Hollingsworth spit out.

"Did something happen I'm not aware of?" Margaret asked, her gaze bouncing between Hollingsworth and me.

"Hollingsworth and Lord Marsh had a bit of disagreement," I explained. "We'd invited Lady Charlotte to accompany us to Gennaro's so she could retrieve the wrap she'd left behind at the club. Lord Marsh roundly objected to, well, me, as well as Hollingsworth. He had some rather choice words for both of us."

"Such as?" Robert's silky voice asked. Whenever it became so, he was at his most dangerous.

"It was nothing, Robert. I forgot about it as soon as I left Marsh House." I hadn't bothered to mention it to him because I hadn't wished to give it any importance. Seemingly, that had been a mistake.

"If you don't tell me, I'll find out another way."

"He said Kitty courted notoriety and she was a walking scandal," Lady Mellie said.

"You weren't there. How could you possibly know?" I asked, much surprised.

Lady Mellie's mischievous smile made an appearance. "A little birdie told me."

My gaze bounced to her brother.

"Don't look at me," Hollingsworth said. "I didn't tell her."

"Neither did I. And we were the only ones there, besides Lord Marsh," I explained.

"You forget Lady Charlotte," Lady Mellie said.

"She told you?" Lady Lily enquired, a befuddled expression on her face. "When?"

"At the Walcott ball, earlier this week. While you were dancing with Ned, she and I enjoyed a comfortable coze.

"What did she say?" I asked.

CHAPTER 26

THE INVESTIGATIVE COMMITTEE MEETS, (PART DEUX)

"WELL, FIRST OF ALL, Lady Charlotte apologized for what Lord Marsh said about Kitty. I thanked her for her kind thought. But I told her there was no need to do so, as she hadn't been the transgressor."

"Just so," Hollingsworth said.

Her mischievous smile grew wider as she looked at Hollingsworth. "And then she asked me to put in a word with you, brother."

Hollingsworth's brow knitted. "Regarding?"

"Becoming part of your crew."

He shot up in his seat. "What? She's a woman."

"Excellent observation, Hollingsworth," Marlowe said, clearly facetiously.

"Oh, hush," Lady Emma chided.

"Children." I clapped to get everyone's attention. "While Lady Charlotte's state of mind is certainly of interest, we can share what she said at a later time. For now we need to focus on Lord Marsh."

"Regarding that," Lady Mellie said. "Apparently, her brother had been in the dumps prior to Lord Rosewood's death. But when he heard about his demise, Lord Marsh turned quite exuberant. Apparently, he now thinks the Lord High Chancellor office is his."

"Not under MacDonald's government, it isn't," Sebastian said. "That office might be appointed by the crown, but it's based on the prime minister's recommendation. MacDonald would never appoint a conservative to Lord High Chancellor. Still, I'll have a word with the Prime Minister to confirm that is so."

"Thank you, Sebastian," I said. "But the question I'd like us to consider is whether he had something to do with Rosewood's death."

Everyone in the room gazed at each other as riotous thoughts raced through their heads. But it took Marlowe to clarify my question. "In other words, did he have Rosewood killed?"

"Surely, he wouldn't commit murder," Lady Lily said. "He has a title, wealth."

"Boundless ambition can drive a man to do unspeakable things," Ned said.

"I don't understand. What's so important about the Lord High Chancellor office?" Lady Lily asked.

"The Lord High Chancellor oversees the courts," Ned explained. "He's also a member of the Privy Council and the Cabinet. The person who holds that office has immense power to affect legislation."

"But according to Sebastian, Prime Minister MacDonald is not likely to appoint Lord Marsh," Lady Lily said.

"You're right. But what if the Labour Party was no longer in power? What if the Conservatives were?"

"Can that happen?"

"All too easily, I'm afraid."

Part and parcel of Ned's responsibilities at Worthington & Son was to be informed about British politics. Any shift in government leadership was likely to impact investment opportunities both at home and abroad.

"If I may explain."

"Of course," I said.

"Ramsay MacDonald, just this year became the first Labour Party Prime Minister. It's up to him to ask the Crown to name a Lord High Chancellor. He would never appoint a conservative such as Lord Marsh. Lord Rosewood, on the other hand, was a liberal. With his pedigree and credentials, he was easily the front-runner. The Labour Party is working on a very ambitious agenda—building municipal houses for low-wage workers, as well as education, unemployment, social insurance measures and tenant protection."

"But those are all good things, aren't they?" Lady Lily asked.

"The Conservatives don't think so. They think the Labour Party has overextended itself. So they're likely to seek a vote of no confidence for MacDonald. If it passes, he would be forced to resign. More than likely, the Conservatives would regain power and appoint a new Prime Minister. That's why Lord Marsh has been wining and dining members of the Conservative Party. So when a Conservative Prime Minister is elected, he would appoint Lord Marsh as the next Lord High Chancellor."

"Thank you for explaining that, Ned," I said. "So, as we see, forces are at work that would change the fortunes of the Lord High Chancellor Office which might very well be given to Lord Marsh. Since Lord Rosewood is no longer a candidate, MacDonald needs to fill that position with another Labour Party member. But it will take time for another one as qualified as Lord Rosewood to rise to the top. As Ned has so eloquently explained, MacDonald might not have that kind of time."

"We don't have a scintilla of evidence connecting Lord Marsh to Rosewood's murder," Robert rightfully pointed out.

For a few moments, silence reigned. And then Lady Mellie spoke out, "Lady Charlotte might have seen something, or heard something. I can bring up the subject at a ball tomorrow night. Hopefully, she will be there."

I hated to involve someone not connected with our committee, mainly because she'd be an unknown quantity. But we had no other option. At least not one I could see.

"Don't pry too much, Lady Mellie. Simply ask if she's seen a stranger or someone who doesn't belong. If she did, get a description and bring it back to us. We can take it from there."

"Very well." Although she'd agreed, she seemed concerned. Had she changed her mind?

"Would you rather not? I can attend the ball and ask her myself, if you wish."

"No. It's not that. Can we revisit the subject of Lady Charlotte?"

"Yes, of course."

"I'm worried about her."

"How so?" Hollingsworth asked.

"Those suppers her uncle is holding? Well, one gentleman has been paying insidious attention to Lady Charlotte. Unwelcome by her, needless to say."

That was very alarming. "Please explain."

"In a couple of instances, he's caught her in a hallway and made quite lewd suggestions."

"Such as?" Hollingsworth asked in a frigid tone. He might not want Lady Charlotte on his ship, but he would never allow her to be dishonored.

"He invited her to join him in the library where they could hold a private chat. She refused, of course."

While Hollingsworth was busy gnashing his teeth, I asked, "Did she inform Lord Marsh?"

"He dismissed her complaints. He's depending on this so-called gentleman's influence to be named Lord High Chancellor. And I'm afraid it's bound to get worse. Marsh will be hosting a shooting party in August at his country estate. He flat out told Lady Charlotte she's to play hostess. And, of course, this gentleman will be invited. The situation has become so untenable she's considering, well, running away."

"Oh, dear," I said. "We can't have that."

"This ball, tomorrow, is it Lady Duquesne's?" Margaret asked.

"Yes," Lady Mellie answered.

"I'll be there. I'll invite her to afternoon tea on Friday at Wynchcombe House. Lord Marsh cannot possibly forbid her from attending. Not when the invitation comes from the Duchess of Wynchcombe."

When it came to protecting women, Margaret wielded her title very effectively, as I had seen her do more than once.

"But what about after the afternoon tea?" Lady Mellie asked.

"I'll think of something," Margaret said. "In the meantime, Hollingsworth you need to ask her to dance at the ball."

"What? Why?"

"You're the only unattached gentleman in our group," Margaret said. "And for some odd reason she seems to like you. Or at least she likes your ship. Regarding the why, she needs to be seen as a lady we value. Your paying attendance to her will clearly convey that message."

"Marsh will have an apoplexy once he sees us dancing."

"Not in public, he won't," Margaret responded. "It would set the tabbies talking, and he needs to maintain a pristine reputation if he wants to be appointed Lord High Chancellor."

"Lady Charlotte may suffer in private," Lady Mellie pointed out.

"I'll have a word with him," Sebastian said. "Make it clear if I see so much as a mark on Lady Charlotte's cheek, he will suffer the consequences."

A knock on the library door preceded the entrance of three footmen carrying trays stacked with sandwiches and pastries plus coffee service for all.

Heavens! Was it three already? I'd asked for refreshments to be served at that time. Just as well. We needed a respite. "Should we take a break? We can resume in fifteen minutes."

While our guests helped themselves to the refreshments, Robert took me aside. "We don't seem to be making much headway."

"They are a bit rusty. Stands to reason. They haven't been part of an investigation since . . ."

A shadow clouded his face. "Oxford."

"Yes." I regretted my comment as it reminded him of a dark part of his life. "And they're busy with their lives. Ladies Lily and Mellie have their season, Hollingsworth, his ship, Margaret, her causes, Lady Emma, the agency. Maybe we're asking too much of them."

"They came here voluntarily," he rightfully pointed out.

"After I begged for their help. Should I say something? That they can bow out if they wish?"

He glanced back at the others who seemed to be enjoying themselves.

"Mention it, but don't force the issue."

I nodded. I would hate to lose any of them. But I would understand if someone decided to step back. Fifteen minutes later, I reconvened the meeting. "Robert and I held a discussion. With everything that's going on in your lives, another investigation might prove too much of an imposition. So, if any wish to bow out, Robert and I will understand."

Dead silence met our announcement. And then Lady Mellie's small voice cried out, "I don't want to bow out. I want to participate. And if we can somehow make Lord Marsh bleed, so much the better." Fire blazed in her eyes when she spoke those last words.

"Bloodthirsty little thing, isn't she?" I whispered beneath my breath to Robert.

"She is Hollingsworth's sister," he replied by way of an explanation.

"None of us want to quit, Kitty," Ned, ever the voice of reason, said. "We all want justice to be done."

"Very well. If everyone feels the same way, we will continue."

Lady Emma raised a hand. "Has anybody talked to Maurice Gautier?"

"I have, of course," Robert said, somewhat affronted.

"You're the law, Sheriff," Hollingsworth offered with a grin. "He wouldn't have responded favorably to your questions, especially after you arrested him. He needs to be questioned by someone more favorably disposed toward him."

"Kitty should talk to him," Lady Emma suggested. "Monique should be present so he knows he can trust her."

"Well, er, Monique is indisposed at the moment," I said.

"What's wrong with her?" Marlowe asked, not unkindly.

"She's exhausted."

"Stands to reason after everything she's gone through," Lady Lily said.

"Well, there's a tad more to it than that." They had to know as there wasn't a prayer in hell of word not getting out. "At yesterday's reading of the will, she revealed Rosewood married her in Paris."

Hollingsworth whistled. "Well, that will set the cat among the pigeons."

"I'm sure it will once the press finds out. The solicitor verified it. Rosewood put the marriage certificate in his keeping."

"The newspapers will crucify her."

"Yes, I fear they will, but that only adds more urgency to our investigation. The sooner we find Rosewood's murderer, the sooner her brother's name will be cleared, and the sooner she can assume a normal life." Normal being relative in her case. Chances were she'd never return to the life she'd once led.

"So what's the plan moving forward?" Lady Emma asked.

"Robert and I will meet with Salverton. Lady Mellie will try to discover more information from Lady Charlotte, and Hollingsworth will dance with her."

Hollingsworth predictably groaned.

"Margaret will hold a tea on Friday, Sebastian will talk to Lord Marsh, and I will question Maurice. I think that about covers it."

As we didn't have a single fact to perch our hat on, all of it was a fishing expedition. But at least we had several avenues to explore.

"We'll meet again on Monday." That would give us time to gather information. Or at least I hoped it would.

CHAPTER 27

A DISCUSSION WITH SALVERTON

*A*FTER THE MEETING ENDED, Robert and I headed to Father's study so he could telephone Salverton. We were fortunate to find him at home. He agreed to meet with us the next day which frankly surprised both Robert and me.

"Do you think he's had a change of heart about discussing things with us?"

"I think the writing's on the wall, and those in command realize they need to give us more information so we can find the murderer. The sooner we do, the sooner the investigation ends. And whatever secrets Rosewood possessed will follow him to the grave."

"Will you join us for supper?"

"Yes, but I have to go home first."

Stood to reason. He would need to change into his formal evening wear.

After saying our goodbyes, I headed upstairs. With any

luck, I could enjoy a bit of rest before dressing for supper. But before I did that, I knocked on Monique's door. Doctor Crawley had arranged for a midwife to call on her, and I wanted to hear how it'd gone. I found her lounging on a chaise lounge, reading a book.

"How did the visit with the midwife go?" I asked.

"Everything's fine," she said with a bright smile. "But she suggested I continue to rest, at least for the time being. And she strongly advised me to stay away from Gennaro's. It might prove too stressful for the baby and me. On a positive note, she approved my joining your family for supper."

"Splendid. We haven't had as much of your company as we wished. Well, I'll leave you to rest."

"Your ceiling fans." She pointed up. "They're a wonder. We had nothing like that back home."

"I believe they're a rather new invention. Father had them installed during the winter. We all appreciate them, especially the staff. Their sleeping quarters are located on the top floor."

"Your family is so thoughtful and kind, Miss Worthington. I don't know what would have happened to me if you hadn't come to my aid."

"We're all glad to do so. Now I really must run. The cocktails' gong will sound before we know it, and I want to get some rest of my own. See you then."

I managed to get a bit of a lie in. So I was quite refreshed when I joined family and friends for supper.

Monique joined us dressed in the stunning gold gown I'd spotted in her dressing room at the club. At first, she hardly spoke. But when Lady Mellie asked about her songs, she opened up. Soon, we were receiving quite an education on jazz and ragtime. Lady Mellie, who'd managed to obtain some sheet music, had been practicing in the music room.

She asked Monique if she would feel comfortable joining her the next day.

"She's supposed to be resting, Lady Mellie," I reminded her.

"Yes, of course," Lady Mellie said, her face pinking up. "My apologies."

"My life has always been filled with music," Monique said. "The last few days not being able to sing, I've missed it. So, yes, Lady Mellie, I'd love to join you."

Lady Mellie tossed her a bright smile. "It's settled then."

"We should do it in the morning before it gets too hot, though."

"Of course."

The following morning the entire house was filled with jazz tunes and songs both joyous and sad. It was no surprise everyone in the house found a reason to go past the music room at one time or another.

Two o'clock found Robert and me at Lord Salverton's residence. Rather than the ubiquitous offer of tea, he offered us a refreshing fruit punch, something I certainly appreciated, the temperature being as hot as it was.

"Our investigation hasn't gotten as far as we wished," I said.

"That's because there's some key information missing."

Just as I thought.

"You need to be informed about Rosewood's intelligence activities."

So, we'd guessed correctly.

"As a chief detective inspector, you would have been sworn to the Official Secrets Act," he said to Robert.

"I have."

"I assume you haven't, Miss Worthington."

"I have not."

"Right. I've been authorized to provide you with information regarding Rosewood's activities in a certain matter. It took some doing. My superiors felt a—"

"Woman?"

Salverton dismissed my comment with a glance. "A *civilian* should not be made privy to highly confidential information. I convinced them otherwise. I reminded them you've kept secret about other national security matters. I sincerely hope my trust in you will be justified."

"It will be."

"In order for me to share this information, I need you to sign this affidavit." He slid a sheet of paper toward me. "Basically, it says that what I'm about to reveal may not be shared with anyone. If you do, the penalty is prison. Do you understand?"

"Y-yes."

After carefully reading the document, I signed it. Robert witnessed my signature.

Salverton rolled up the single sheet and stuffed it into a thick envelope which he locked in a valise. "I will deliver this document to the proper authorities. It will be on file with them until the end of time. If another confidential matter surfaces that you're made privy to, the same terms apply. Do you understand?"

"I wouldn't have to sign anything again?"

"No. Once is enough."

"But what if I discover confidential information accidentally?"

"You're not likely to." He sighed. "But if you do, you are to notify me. I will take it from there. Anything else?"

"No. Thank you for trusting me."

"You're welcome. Now regarding Lord Rosewood. Are you familiar with the Committee of Imperial Defense?"

Robert, of course, knew. I, on the other hand, had never heard of it.

"That body researches, and provides, some co-ordination on issues of military strategy. Temporary sub-committees are set up to investigate and report at length on a specific topic. Recently, a records leak was discovered regarding one of those topics. It was noticed when someone requested a document and found it missing. An exhaustive search was conducted. But after two weeks, it could not be located."

"I'm guessing that document was very important."

"Yes, it was. We have three document classifications—confidential, highly confidential, and top secret. The higher the level, the more stringent standards. That particular document was classified as confidential." He paused for a moment. "Any questions so far?"

"Where are the documents kept?" Robert asked.

"In a highly secured location."

"Not secure enough if somebody waltzed in and stole one," I said.

"Fair enough."

"Who has direct access to those documents?"

"A dozen or so clerks who are assigned to that unit. As you can imagine once we discovered the document had gone missing, we focused on those individuals. One became a person of interest. He'd been in debt up to his ears. But suddenly it was paid off."

"He was bribed," I said.

"That's what we believe. Unfortunately, before we could bring him in for questioning, he was found with his throat slashed."

"Dead men tell no tales," Robert said.

"Just so. Suspecting a particular foreign operative was involved, we kept a close eye on him."

"Why didn't you arrest him?"

"We can't arrest an individual unless we have proof of wrongdoing. We had none. But then he made arrangements to travel to France. Unusual. He hadn't left England for over a year. We tailed him as far as Calais, but then we lost him. He must have realized he was being followed. But we knew he was headed for Paris.

I hissed in a breath. "That's why Rosewood was there."

"Yes. He knew the foreign operative by sight. Problem was we didn't know who he'd be meeting or when. But we'd discovered their rendezvous point."

"The cabaret where Monique was singing."

"Exactly so."

"So, Lord Rosewood cooled his heels in the cabaret waiting for the operative to arrive. During that time, he fell in love with Monique."

Salverton nodded. "After a month in Paris, we decided something had gone wrong. More than likely, the operative had been replaced. If that was the case, Rosewood would not recognize the substitute. He was about to return to London when the man we'd been tailing finally showed up. Rosewood bided his time waiting for the exchange. When it happened, the French Gendarme police arrested both operatives. They'd been lying in wait along with Rosewood. The foreign operative, a British national, was escorted back to England where, let's just say, he met swift justice."

"There was nothing about it in the papers," I said.

"The British government can't very well admit its security measures were not quite what they should be."

"What was the document's final destination?" I asked.

"Berlin."

"The Great War never really ended, did it?" I asked.

"The war did, the conflict between our two countries has not."

"But if the foreign operative was caught and the clerk was killed, why did someone murder Rosewood?" Robert asked.

"Because there's a third party involved. And it can only be

someone who works for the Committee of Imperial Defense," Salverton declared.

"How do you figure that?" I asked.

"Clerks can retrieve documents, but they can't remove them. To ensure compliance, they're all thoroughly searched before exiting the premises."

"So the clerk who retrieved the confidential document would have handed it to someone who works for the Committee," Robert said.

"Exactly."

"Any idea who?" I asked.

"Could be anyone. As long as that individual has clearance, all he needs to do is complete a form. The clerk fetches the document requested and hands it to him."

"But wouldn't the record reflect who asked for that particular document?"

"The person named in the record does not exist."

"That seems to be a flaw in the system," I said.

"You're correct. We've taken steps to ensure that doesn't happen again."

"That particular document may never have reached the German Reich," Robert said, "but you still have to apprehend the person who works for the committee."

"Yes." Salverton took to pacing the floor, much as he had done the last time I met with him. "Unfortunately, during our search, we discovered an additional document was missing. A top-secret one, so sensitive that if it fell into the wrong hands, it might precipitate another European conflict."

"And you still don't know who he is?" Robert asked.

"No. During our investigation we identified another foreign agent. Through exhaustive means, we learned that he wanted to get out of the spy business. Things were getting too dangerous for him. But he needed money to do that. We were willing to pay as long as we could identify the traitor at the Committee of Imperial Defense. After the Paris operation failed, he was told to lie low and await instructions as to the time and place where the next exchange would take place. And then he finally heard from his superiors. The top-secret document was to be transferred to him right here in London."

"At Gennaro's the night Rosewood was murdered."

"Right. Rosewood knew what the foreign agent looked like. We'd pointed him out when we brought in the agent to work out the details."

"So that night, Rosewood would have witnessed the exchange, maybe even recognized the turncoat."

"I believe so. We had agents posted throughout the club. All he needed to do was point out the traitor, and we would have arrested him. Unfortunately, Rosewood was killed before he could pass on the information. I'll never under-stand why he didn't alert us right away."

"He was worried about Monique, Lord Salverton," I said. "The woman he loved. His wife. He wanted to get her to safety before he informed your agents."

"We didn't know they were married. I thought"— he brushed fingers across his brow —"I thought she was just his *chère amie.*"

"She was so much more than that," I said.

It took Robert to recall us to the here and now. "So the killer did not enter through the bathroom window in the green room or the storage area. He was there all the time. Unfortunately, we have no way of knowing who it is."

"But somebody else does," I said.

"Who?"

"A member of the jazz band. One of them had to tell the murderer about Maurice Gautier's revolver. Otherwise, how would he know it was there?"

"You're right," Robert said. "We need to question every member of the band, starting with August Baudet."

A gleeful smile rolled across Salverton's face. "I'll be there with the thumb screws."

Goodness! I wouldn't want to be in August's shoes.

CHAPTER 28

QUESTIONING MAURICE

*T*HE FOLLOWING MORNING while Robert and Salverton carried out their plans, Monique and I made our way to King's Hospital. After several days of rest, she was feeling better and very much wished to see her brother.

We found him not only awake but alert. His physician happened to be in the room assessing his vitals. A happy coincidence because he was able to provide Monique with his prognosis—Maurice was out of danger, but his road to recovery would take several weeks. And then he provided extensive details of what she could expect.

Monique was so happy to see her brother smiling, I didn't think most of his words registered with her. But I took note, so I could repeat them back to her. The physician did not remain long. He had other patients to see. Neither did the matron who followed him out of the room. But before she left, she cautioned us not to spend much time. Maurice tired easily, and he needed his rest. We promised to keep our visit short.

Carefully embracing her brother, Monique kissed him on the cheek. His brilliant smile echoed her joy. The two of them may have been at odds over Lord Rosewood, but it was clear they cared strongly for one another.

Proof of that was his first question to her. "How are you, Moni?"

"I'm fine, dear brother." She squeezed his hand. "I'm living at Worthington House now. They're taking very good care of me."

His brow furrowed. "Why is that?"

"Inspector Crawford Sinclair did not think it safe to remain at the Merton Park house after what happened to you."

A shadow fell over his face.

"You are not to think about that place, *chere*," Monique gently chided. "You won't be going back."

He started to shake his head but thought better of it. "You don't know that."

Monique turned to me. "Can you explain it to him?"

"Of course," I said stepping forward. I'd remained in the background to allow them a moment of privacy.

"Maury, this is Miss Worthington. She's the lady detective I hired to investigate . . . George's death."

"How do you do, Mister Gautier?" Hard to believe this was the first time I was meeting him.

His brow furrowed. "Is what Moni says true? I won't be taken back to prison?"

Of course, I couldn't assert that, so I phrased it as positively as I could. "Things are looking promising in that regard."

"How?"

"Scotland Yard has reopened the investigation into Lord Rosewood's murder."

Monique hitched a breath. "I'm sorry. Go on, Miss Worthington."

I nodded. "After you were assaulted, Scotland Yard came to realize you're not responsible for his death."

His upper lip curled with derision. "I told the cop that. He didn't believe me."

"Maury. That cop is Miss Worthington's fiancé. He's fighting for you as much as she is." I'd shared with her the progress of our investigation. Granted it was little enough, but it'd allowed her to hope.

"Mister Gautier, we don't have much time, and I have a few questions. May I ask them? Your answers may help us discover the one responsible."

Unsmiling, he nodded.

Flipping open my notebook, I chose the five most important ones. If I had sufficient time, I would ask the rest.

"Regarding your gun case, I was told you kept it in the cabinet in the men's dressing area."

"That's right."

"Who knew about it?"

"All the members of the band."

"What about Gennaro's staff?"

"I doubt they knew. They weren't allowed in the men's dressing area."

That was rather odd. "Not even to clean?"

"We tidied the area ourselves. Any trash we had we put in the green room before we left for the night."

"Why the secrecy?"

"We stored our instruments in the dressing area. As valuable as they are, King didn't want anyone but us in there. He kept the room locked overnight."

I made a note of that. "Was the room locked while you were performing?"

"No. We were in and out of the dressing room each night. That's where we kept our wallets, cigarettes . . . other things. It would have been too much trouble to ask King for the key every time."

"So somebody could have gone into the men's dressing area while the band was playing and taken your weapon."

He thought about it for a couple of moments. "I suppose someone could have entered the room, but my gun case was locked."

"Where did you keep that key?"

"On me, attached to a key chain."

"And yet, the revolver was stolen."

He huffed out a breath. "Yes."

"How do you explain it?"

"I can't. If I had been given a chance to examine the gun case, maybe I could've explained it. But I did not have the opportunity as I was immediately arrested."

By Robert. He would have taken Mister Gautier to Scotland Yard, a much better place to interrogate a suspect. Didn't fault him for doing so. It was standard operating procedure, after all. "Is there another key?"

"I had a duplicate in my wallet."

"Which you kept in the cabinet."

"Yes. We all kept our wallets there."

"So arguably somebody could have opened the cabinet, searched your wallet, located the key to the gun case, and taken the revolver."

He frowned. "That must be how it happened. But it doesn't make any sense. How would they know about the gun and the key?"

"All the band members knew."

"Yes, but—"

Unfortunately, he wasn't able to finish his thought. The matron had reentered the room. "I'm sorry, but Mister Gautier needs his rest."

"Yes, of course," Monique said and pressed another kiss on her brother's cheek. "I'll come back tomorrow."

"You don't have to, Moni. Now that I know you're in a good place, I can rest easy."

Neville had driven us to the hospital with the police officer sitting in front. So on the way back we couldn't discuss what we'd learned. But after we arrived at Worthington House, I followed her to her room. There we could hold our conversation in private. "One of the band members may be connected to the theft of the revolver."

She gazed at me out of sad eyes. "Yes."

"Any idea who?"

She didn't hesitate for a second. "August. He gambles. Loses all the time. King was reluctant to hire him. But just before we left for Paris, our piano player quit. So he had to find a fast replacement. August's reputation preceded him, but King had no choice."

"I'll let Robert know." I pressed her hands. "Try not to worry."

She offered me a sad smile. "Easier said than done."

I made my way to the study to telephone Robert. Unfortunately, he wasn't available. Made sense. He was probably rounding up the members of the jazz band and bringing them in for questioning. After leaving word for him to call me, I made my way to my room to change into my afternoon clothes. I had Margaret's tea to attend.

CHAPTER 29

AFTERNOON TEA AT THE DUCHESS OF
WYNCHCOMBE'S

*L*ADIES LILY, MELLIE, EMMA AND I arrived at
Wynchcombe House in the Worthington Rolls
Royce. Heaven forfend we travel in my roadster.
One had to arrive in style at a duke's address, didn't you
know?

Even among all the other great houses of Mayfair, the
mansion was an imposing presence. Built by an earlier duke
during the Georgian period, it stood three stories high with
wings flaring out on each side and a myriad of large
windows lining its front.

While Mister Temple, the Wynchcombe butler, escorted
us to our destination, I once again marveled at the transfor-
mation Lady Lily had wrought. The former furniture with its
heavy moldings and twisted and elaborate motifs had been
rather stodgy. But Sebastian's grandfather had had no

interest in refurbishing the mansion and kept it exactly as it'd existed for two hundred years.

Before his marriage to my sister, Sebastian had given his sister carte blanche to bring the furnishings up to snuff. Something Margaret had thoroughly approved of, as she didn't care two figs for redecoration. Consequently, Lady Lily had replaced the ornate, baroque-style furnishings with more delicate Queen Anne pieces. She'd also covered the walls with fresh new designs and hung drapes to match. As a result, the rooms, which now reflected Sebastian's, Lily's, and Margaret's vibrant youth, were absolutely charming.

Upon our arrival at the drawing room, Margaret welcomed us warmly. But then, she could do no less. She was our mother's daughter after all.

While we were greeting each other, Lady Delphine arrived. I hadn't seen her since my birthday celebration three weeks before, so I was eager to learn how she was faring. In previous years, she'd endured three seasons of being paraded like a prize mare in search of a stallion. But this year had been different. She'd outright refused to participate in another one as her dream was to open a modiste shop in the heart of London.

Her mother disapproved of the notion. Daughters of the nobility did not engage in trade. But after talking to Margaret, who'd employed quite brilliant marriage proposal avoidance maneuvers during her own debut, Lady Delphine agreed to one last season. But only if her mother agreed to her proposal. If she didn't receive one acceptable offer of marriage, she would be allowed to open her shop. Since Lady Delphine's father had already approved the scheme, her mother was forced to agree.

Lady Charlotte, the last to arrive, apologized profusely for being a tad late. As she didn't trust her uncle, Lord

Marsh, to put a stop to her outing, she waited until he left the house.

As soon as she entered the drawing room, Mister Temple proceeded with the tea service. The elaborate spread consisted of tea, scones, assorted cakes and pastries, accompanied by delicate porcelain cups and plates. In no time at all, laughter was ringing out while we discussed the latest fashion, gossip, and, of course, those human foibles which made life enjoyable.

"So how is the husband avoidance plan coming along?" I asked Lady Delphine when I sat next to her. Taking a leaf from Margaret's debut season, Lady Delphine had made herself as undesirable a wife as possible. If an interested gentleman liked the country, she said she fancied the city. If he enjoyed merrymaking, she confessed to preferring a quiet life. If a gentleman was looking for a broodmare, she'd declared her distaste for children.

"Excellently," she said. "Haven't received a single proposal. I'm so optimistic of the outcome, I'm looking at properties for my modiste shop."

"Do you have a particular area in mind?"

"Bond Street. I admit the lease cost will be a trifle high, but hopefully I can attract the sort of clientele who appreciate haute couture designed for ladies to wear in professional settings."

"That sounds downright marvelous, Lady Delphine. I'll be one of your first clients."

"I was hoping you'd say that. I intend to hold a fashion show of my spring collection at the Ritz in September."

"Oh, we all will attend. Won't we, ladies?"

Not everyone had been listening in on our conversation, so of course I had to explain. But when they heard, they were totally on board.

"Unfortunately, I won't be able to make it," Lady Charlotte said rather forlornly. "My uncle has planned a number of house parties for August and September at Exeter Castle, and he wants me there to play hostess for him."

"I'm afraid you won't be able to take on that role, Lady Charlotte," Margaret said.

Lady Charlotte gazed at her somewhat confused. "Why not?"

"Why, you'll be coming with us to Brighton. In August, we'll be there for two weeks. You will also be joining us in September."

Getting into the spirit of the thing, Lady Charlotte grinned. "Pray tell what will I be doing instead?"

"You'll be attending an intimate Harvest celebration at Wynchcombe Castle. Since you and I are bosom bows, I couldn't possibly abide your not being there."

"Bosom bows?" Lady Charlotte laughed gaily. "We're barely acquainted."

"Well, my dear, we have two months to change that. From now until the end of the season, we'll be seen chatting at every ball, every theatre outing that we both attend. We'll need to coordinate schedules, of course. By the time August arrives, Marsh won't dare question your friendship with the Duchess of Wynchcombe. Not as much as he wants to curry favor with members of the House of Lords."

Lady Charlotte grew serious. "You'd do that? For me? Why?"

"I hate bullies, and your uncle, Lady Charlotte, is very much one. I mean to have his nose good and bloodied, figuratively speaking of course, by the time we're through with him."

"We?"

"We're all in, especially Lady Mellie." I nodded toward her. "I think she wants to draw blood in person."

"I certainly do," Lady Mellie stated firmly. "Nobody

insults my brother and my very good friend without suffering consequences."

A smiling Lady Charlotte glanced around the room. "What did I do to gain such great friends?"

"We're the sisterhood of women," Margaret said. "One for all and all for one. That's our motto."

The rest of the afternoon passed very pleasantly, but, like all good things, it eventually came to an end.

"I hate to return to Marsh House after such a convivial afternoon," Lady Charlotte said.

"Your uncle isn't treating you . . . unkindly, is he?" I asked.

"No more than usual. As you saw when you visited, he loves to issue edicts to those he considers inferior to him. As much as possible, I give him a wide berth. Nicky, however, does not."

"Nicky?" I asked.

"The Honorable Nicholas Derwent," she said, "Marsh's third son and my cousin. They've been at odds with each other for the longest time."

"Any particular reason?"

"He's always begging his father to increase his allowance which Marsh refuses to do. He never seems to have a feather to fly with. Why, at Gennaro's we had to depend on my allowance to pay for our drinks."

"He was at Gennaro's?" I asked.

"You met him, Kitty," Lady Emma said. "When you returned from tripping the light fantastic with Inspector Crawford Sinclair. He was the chap talking to Marlowe. He introduced you."

When I still couldn't recall, she said, "Dark haired, blue eyed, tall."

Light finally dawned. "Oh, that gentleman! Marlowe did mention he was a fribble."

"I love Nicky dearly," Lady Charlotte said, "but I understand why he's perceived in such a manner. He doesn't take life as seriously as he should. When he came of age three years ago, Marsh encouraged him to join the military. He refused. So Marsh got him appointed as an aide to one of his friends. At the Committee of Imperial Defense, if you can believe it."

My coffee cup rattled so much I had to set it down in a hurry. "Interesting."

"He's rubbish at it, according to Marsh. So much so, he's in danger of losing his position. If he's dismissed, Marsh told Nicky not to count on him for support. He can bloody well live on the streets. Excuse my language. I'm only repeating what Marsh said."

Margaret accompanied us to the front of the house where we all said our goodbyes. As Neville drove us back to Worthington House, I stopped myself from asking him to drive faster.

CHAPTER 30

A DISCUSSION WITH MARLOWE

*A*S SOON AS I ARRIVED HOME, I telephoned Robert. Again! But he still wasn't available. As patience was not a virtue I had ever possessed, I reached out to the one person who was acquainted with Nicholas Derwent—Lord Marlowe. Thankfully, he was at home. Without bothering to change from my afternoon togs, I jumped in my roadster and drove to his home.

"What on earth has you in such a lather?" He asked when I was shown into his study.

"I think Nicholas Derwent is the murderer!"

"Nicky? All he cares about is enjoying himself. Why do you think that?"

I couldn't tell him as I had sworn I wouldn't reveal what I'd learned from Salverton. "I can't say. I'm sorry. I shouldn't have come. But I couldn't reach Robert, and I needed to do something. I should go." Heavens, I was babbling.

"Don't. Give me a minute to think it through." He bowed his head, seemingly deep in thought.

I waited. Nothing else I could do.

His gaze found me. "He was at Gennaro's that night."

I nodded.

"He's involved in something; otherwise he would not have killed Rosewood. But what?" He drummed fingers across his cheek. "He works for the Committee of Imperial Defense as an aide to one of the advisory members. Someone in the military. Salverton somehow is involved, and rumor has it he works for MI-6. His travels abroad to buy rare stamps provide cover." He snapped his fingers. "Nicky must be involved in some sort of espionage." His face lost all its humor. "Against the British government! The blighter."

I said nothing. I didn't even blink. I had to admit he was very good at this.

He gazed pointedly at me. "We have to do something."

"We can't go off half-cocked, Marlowe. Robert must be told."

Ignoring me, he glanced at the mantel clock. "It's half past five. He might be at White's."

When he headed toward the door, I barred his way. "You can't do this."

"You don't know what I'm going to do."

"Beat him to a pulp."

He blew out a breath. "Lucky guess." A thought suddenly occurred to him. "How did he obtain the revolver?"

I explained my theory.

"Whoever that person was, he needs to be questioned."

"Robert and Salverton are doing that."

The doorknob rattled behind me. "Catherine, are you there?"

I jumped away from the portal. "Robert!"

"How did he know where you were?" Marlowe asked.

"I left word at home." I swung round and opened the study door.

"What are you doing here?" Robert asked.

"No time to explain. It's Nicky Derwent. Marsh's son."

"How did you discover that?"

I told him what Lady Charlotte had said at Margaret's afternoon tea.

"It fits, Sinclair," Marlowe said.

"Did you tell him?" He nodded toward the earl.

"No. He guessed. He's very good at it."

"While you stand there arguing, Derwent might slip through our fingers," Marlowe pointed out.

"Do you know where he is?" Robert asked.

"White's. He's usually there Saturday afternoons. His flat is close to the club."

Robert lowered his brows. "You seem unusually knowledgeable about his comings and goings."

"He's always caching invitations from one member or another as he can't afford to pay for things himself. Nicky's always up for a lark as long as someone else is footing the bill. He gets invited to suppers, card parties, and, er, other forms of entertainment."

"The risqué sort?" I asked.

"Yes.'

"Anything special going on tonight?" Robert asked.

"Lord Wallace is holding an exclusive gathering at his house in Woolwich."

"That's a bit of a stretch from London," I said.

"Eleven, twelve miles as the crow flies."

Robert arched a brow. "Been there, have you?"

"Once." He shrugged. "I was curious."

I propped both fists on my hips. "What exactly goes on at these gatherings?"

"Nothing you need to concern yourself with," Marlowe said.

"Were you invited to tonight's event?" Robert asked.

"Always am."

"Can you bring a guest?" Robert again.

"The more the merrier as far as Wallace is concerned."

"I'm coming as well," I said.

"No. Kitty. You cannot come," Marlowe firmly stated.

"Why not?"

"Because only gentlemen are invited."

"Women must be present for the sort of thing I imagine goes on. What are they? Window dressing?"

"More like undressing," Marlowe said with a grin.

"What time is the event?" Robert asked.

"Ten to dawn."

"I'll need to make arrangements. I'll meet you back here at nine," Robert said. "Come, Catherine. We're leaving."

Not giving me a choice, he took my hand. Before I knew it, we were making our way back to Worthington House in my roadster.

"You are to stay put, Catherine."

I maintained my eyes on the road. Driving took all my attention.

"Are you listening?" He asked.

"I haven't lost my hearing faculty, Robert. Of course, I heard you." I made a quick turn which tossed him sideways.

"Do you always drive like a madwoman?" He asked hanging on to his hat.

"Only when I'm being lectured." I tossed him a feral smile.

"Two police officers are posted at your residence. They'll be keeping their eye on you."

That's what he thought.

CHAPTER 31

THE HOUSE OF EARTHLY DELIGHTS

"*B*ACK DOOR," the guard standing outside Lord Wallace's Woolwich house said. I had to agree he was perfect for the job. Broad, tall, mean-looking. The snarl on his lips would have frightened small children.

But not me. "Ta!" Supremely confident in the part I was playing, I swung my hips side to side as I headed toward the rear of Wallace's Georgian mansion.

Only someone who knew me well would recognize me. Monique had helped me dress the part and apply liberal maquillage. And Claudine had dressed my hair, or rather undressed it.

"Mussed up, that's what the gentlemen like. Like you're ready to party, if you take my meaning."

"You seem to know a lot about this, Claudine," I said.

She seemed somewhat offended. "I was young once, Miss."

"And so you were. Carry on, then."

"Are you sure you should be doing this, Miss Worthington?" Monique asked, her hands twisting with worry. "I appreciate your efforts on our behalf, but you're an innocent. Anyone can see that."

"Now, Miss Monique," Claudine said, "you know that will work in her favor. Some gentlemen like that wide-eyed look."

"But she might find herself in a situation she can't control."

Clearly, I would need to convince her I'd be in no danger. Turning toward her, I held her hands. "Dear Monique, I've trained in martial arts. Tae Kwon Do to be exact. I know the weakest part of a man's body, and I have absolutely no problem applying force to it if need be."

Although her worry had lessened, it hadn't totally dissipated. But I'd had no more time to totally convince her. So I'd said my goodbyes and taken the back stairs to the kitchen, silent and empty as everyone had retired to their quarters. And then in the dark of night, I made my way to the mews in the back of the house, while Robert's police officers watched the front.

Of course, I hadn't traveled to Woolwich by myself. Mister Clapham had come along as well. This wasn't the first foray we'd gone on together, and I absolutely trusted him with my life.

Even as I made my way to the rear, I heard him questioned by the same guard. "Oy! 'Oo are you?"

"Charley Sykes."

"Never 'eard of ye."

"You're not supposed to."

"Wot's an old geezer loike you doing 'ere?"

"It's called experience, my lad. What I know you haven't heard of yet."

"Not bloody likely." He gestured with his thumb. "Back of the 'ouse."

As he caught up to me, I said, "He bought your act."

"I flashed my weapon. That's all it took. It's not too late to back out," he suggested.

"I won't. Marlowe and Robert can't be everywhere."

He heaved a heavy sigh. But he stopped trying to convince me. "That hair. Never seen it before."

I patted my tussled bob, one of the wigs I kept on hand at the agency. "I've always wanted to be a redhead." And then we reached the back door, and there was no more time to talk.

"Name?" The back door guard asked. Not quite as broad or tall as the one in the front, he was still a force to be reckoned with.

I flashed him a smile. "Bee Snees."

"Roight." He masticated his chew of tobacco for a second before spitting to the side. "What's yer game?"

I batted my lashes. "Whatever you want it to be."

"What's with the toff accent?"

"I used to work as a nanny."

He flashed his thumb up. "Romper room."

Not what I expected. "What?"

"Second floor. That's where the babies are." When I didn't move, he ordered, "Well, go on."

"Yes, sir."

Inside I waited for Clapham. "They have babies here? That's despicable."

"Not babies. Grown men dressed as infants."

My jaw dropped. "You're joking."

"Wish I was. They like to be fed, spanked, have their nappies changed."

My stomach heaved. "Oh, for the love of—I'm not doing that."

"You the entertainment?" A man wearing a red bow tie asked.

"Yes, yes, I am." Anything was better than changing a grown man's nappies.

"Dancer, singer—"

I struck a pose. "Dancer."

His gaze raked over me. "A little overdressed, aren't you?"

It was my most daring frock, but seemingly it didn't show enough skin for him. "The fringe is intended to tease a gentleman."

He shrugged. "Whatever you say. Main room straight ahead."

I turned to wait for Mister Clapham, but red tie was giving him a hard time.

"You're not on the list. You ain't a copper, are you?"

"Do I look like one?"

Mister Clapham had glued on a scraggly beard and added a nasty-looking scar.

"No."

"How about you let me get on with the job and stop jabbering at me then?"

"Right. Follow Miss Bee Snees over there. I 'ave a feeling she's going to cause a ruckus."

Mister Clapham saluted red tie. "Whatever you say, Guv."

We walked into the main room where a party was in full swing. An all-woman band, skimpily dressed, was playing on a makeshift stage. Women dressed in flapper outfits were dancing the Charleston. Some had cozied up to a couple of gentlemen and were giving them—goodness—lap dances. I gulped. I sincerely hoped I wouldn't be required to do that. If Robert found out . . . I couldn't finish the thought as somebody slapped my behind.

I turned around. Red tie.

"What are ye waiting for? An invitation?"

"Course not." I grinned at him. If there was something I could dance to, it was the Charleston. Swinging my hands in the air and kicking my heels, I made my entrance. The gentlemen hooted, hollered, and yelled out words, half of which I didn't understand. Going by the glassy look in their eyes, they'd already had quite a bit to drink.

"Go on, dolly, flash those legs."

At least those I understood. Grinning, I kicked my legs some more. Not to be outdone, one of the other dancers turned around and lifted her skirt. My goodness. She had no knickers. Well, when in Rome. My knickers were flesh colored. But as bosky as they were, they wouldn't notice the difference. One of the gentlemen, grabbed a dancer and pulled her to his lap. The woman giggled all the while he stuffed pound notes down her cleavage, stole kisses and pushed his hands up her legs all the way up to—heavens!

I was trying to keep my distance but somehow one grabbed me and pulled me to his lap. A big beefy hand made its way to my derriere. I was just about to tell him to keep his paws off me when my gaze clashed with the brute's.

Robert! In his guise as Jeremiah Bloodsworth. I was truly in the soup.

"What are you doing here?" He gritted out through clenched teeth.

Goodness, he was furious. "Same thing you are."

"Give it to her good and proper, mate," somebody yelled.

Robert ground his mouth against mine with a ferocity I'd never experienced before. I was so surprised, I started to jump to my feet. But he pushed me back down.

"That's right. Show her who's master."

After another mind-numbing kiss, he clutched me by the waist and came to his feet. "This place got any private rooms?" He asked red bow tie.

"Upstairs, second floor. You got twenty minutes. That's when the next show starts."

"What's your name?" Robert asked in his gruff voice.

I hitched up my chin. "Bee Snees."

"Well, Miss Snees, you and I are going to have a bit of fun."

I gulped. What was he going to do?

With me stumbling behind him, he climbed the stairs and opened one door. When someone screamed, he opened the next. Same thing. The third room was empty. He dragged me in there and locked the door behind me. "Scream."

"What?"

"Scream. I want them to think you're having a good time."

I did as he said but the scream barely made it past my lips.

With a crooked smile, he said, "You got to do better than that, Bee!"

"I don't know if I can."

He removed his belt.

"Wh-what are you going to do?"

He smacked the door with the belt.

This time my scream was good and loud.

Somebody pounded on the door. "Oy, mate! Don't damage the goods. She still has to dance."

Robert swung open the door. "Mind your own bloody business, mate."

Red bow tie raised his hands in surrender. "All right. All right." And then he wandered off.

Robert locked the door once more.

"Well, that was exciting," I said.

"What you should be is scared." He curled his hand around my cheek. "You shouldn't have come, Catherine."

"You locked me out, Inspector. Of everything you were going to do."

"There was no time to explain. I had to return to Scotland Yard and set up a surveillance unit."

"They're here?"

"Of course, they are. You don't think I came by myself. We need to capture Derwent. There are men in every room."

"Including the Romper Room?" I asked with a wink.

"Know about that, do you?"

"I do now," I said plopping on the bed. "Where's Marlowe?"

"Looking for Derwent. He knows him personally so he can easily identify him. The police officers only have his description."

"He could slip through your fingers."

"He won't. If a police officer sees him, he's to blow a whistle. Other agents are posted outside. Salverton is in charge out there."

"Is Derwent here already?"

"If he isn't, he should arrive soon."

"You know his movements."

Robert nodded. "He was indeed at White's. An officer outside followed him to his flat. As late as nine, Derwent hadn't left it. I expect he's on his way here right now. He's being followed."

"Won't he notice?"

"It's dark. And there's more than one motorcar. They're switching off leads." He gave me a swift kiss on the lips. "I have to leave you. Lock the door behind me. Don't let anybody in, except for me or Marlowe."

"What about red bow tie? He expects me downstairs for the next show."

"I'll talk to him. You won't be disturbed." He walked out, leaving me to cool my heels. The temptation to head back downstairs was great. But I wouldn't. He had enough officers. Surely, one of them would capture Derwent. Giving in to the inevitable, I lay down and closed my eyes.

I awoke to the sound of someone in the room. How could that be? I'd locked the door.

"Well, well, well, Sleeping Beauty is awake." Tall, blue-eyed, a smirk on his lips.

I knew exactly who he was. "Derwent."

"In the flesh."

"How did you get in?"

"This house has a labyrinth of tunnels that you can enter from every room." He swung a pistol at me. "Get up. You're coming with me."

"Where?"

"You'll see."

CHAPTER 32

A RUN FOR THE COAST

*H*E HELD THE GUN TO MY BACK while we moved through the tunnels and down the stairs. As much as I wished to escape, I didn't even try. If I made the wrong move, he might very well pull the trigger. Besides, the tunnels were so narrow, there was no room to maneuver. After what seemed like forever, we emerged into what I assumed was the basement. Boxes were piled up willy-nilly, and the space gave off an earthy smell.

Drilling the gun into my back, he urged me forward until we reached a door on the other side of the room. Opening the scarred, wooden portal, he pushed me forward. "Go on."

Silently, we made our way through yet another tunnel. This one, unlike the others, had no stairs, although it curved now and again. Finally after what seemed like forever, we climbed a set of steps, five of them, and emerged into the night.

Once more, he drilled the gun into my back. "Keep walking."

I turned around. The back of Lord Wallace's mansion was very far away. "We're going the wrong way, aren't we? The road's in the other direction."

He smirked. "We're not headed for the road."

I stumbled my way across the field, all the while wondering if Robert had realized I'd been kidnapped. Surely, he would have checked on my wellbeing. After twenty minutes or so, we reached a body of water which could only be the Thames. What was he planning to do? Drown me. By God, if he tried to do so, I would not make it easy for him. If I were to die, I'd make sure he did as well.

But apparently, that was not his purpose. At least for the moment. He'd been headed for a motorboat. And someone else was there. Lady Charlotte!

She was spitting mad. Not that she could say anything. He'd not only tied her up but gagged her as well.

"Get in," Derwent said to me.

I had no choice but to climb aboard.

He walked up to Lady Charlotte and held the gun to her head. "Miss Worthington is going to untie your hands and your feet. If either you or her try anything, I'll shoot you both."

"They'll hear the shots back at the house," I said.

"Doubt it. We're too far away. And even if they do, they'll think it's an automobile backfiring." He waved the gun at me. "Now untie her."

I did as I was told. What else could I do? Once I was done, he had Lady Charlotte tie me up. He didn't gag me, though. Made sense. If we were too far away from the house for a shot to be heard, my screams wouldn't be either.

"Nicky, you're beyond despicable," Lady Charlotte said.

"Been called worse. By my own father, no less."

"How did you get here, Lady Charlotte?" I had to learn as much information as I could. If for no other reason, than it might help us escape.

"He kidnapped me. Forced me to maneuver this motorboat."

"Where did you get it?" I asked her cousin.

"Stole it." He waved the gun at Lady Charlotte. "Get this thing going. I haven't got all night."

"I have to hook a fresh petrol supply to the motor."

"Get on with it then."

While Lady Charlotte was busy doing that, I asked, "What are you going to do? Kill us both?"

His smirk was clearly visible from the light of a full moon. "If I have to."

As long as he was talking, I might as well ask, "You killed Rosewood, didn't you?"

"He recognized me, damn his eyes, as I passed a top-secret document to a foreign agent. Thought I was done for. But he chose not to alert the police who was most surely there. At least not for that moment. More than likely, he wanted to get his mistress out of harm's way. Once I realized that, I made my way backstage. I knew where a revolver was kept back there. So I retrieved it."

"How did you know about that?"

"One of the jazz band players, August somebody, was at a gambling den I visited. He blabbed about the band and the wondrous Monique. Kept talking about Maurice and how he had a revolver. Thought the man would use it one day to kill Rosewood. He even revealed where the key to the gun was kept. It was exactly where he said. Americans like to brag about such things. Such fools they are."

Americans were not the only ones. Whether he realized it or not, he was doing that as well right now.

"So, what did you do after you fetched the gun?"

"I hid in the storage room beneath the stage and waited."

"How did you know Rosewood would come backstage?"

"The piano player. Apparently, after the end of every performance Rosewood would meet the singer in her dressing room and then take her home. He bought her a house at Merton Park. Can you believe it?"

"Yes, I can."

"You done with the petrol yet, Charlie?" He asked Lady Charlotte.

"Almost," she answered. "It's tricky." She was keeping him talking. That's what she was doing.

"Maurice Gautier was blamed for the murder," I said.

"There was bad blood between him and Rosewood. Made sense he'd be the natural suspect. After all, it was his gun. Once they arrested him, they would stop looking for someone else."

"And then you bribed a guard to kill Mister Gautier at Brixton Prison. Because once he was dead, the investigation would stop."

He laughed. "That wasn't me. That was dear Papa. Somehow, he figured out I was stealing documents from the Committee of Imperial Defense. He couldn't afford a family scandal as it would scuttle his plans to become the next Lord High Chancellor. So he bribed a Brixton guard to pass a knife to one of the prisoners."

"Maurice ended up in a hospital with life-threatening injuries."

"But he's not dead, and that's what Marsh wanted."

"You're disgusting, Nicky," Lady Charlotte yelled back at him.

"Shut up. Get the boat going. That petrol should be hooked up by now."

Having stalled long enough, Lady Charlotte started the

motor. She then took up the tiller and pointed the boat toward deeper water.

"Where are we headed?" I asked, trying hard not to be tossed about. There wasn't much I could do, though, tied up as I was.

"France."

"On this tiny boat? It'll never make it across the channel."

"Oh, not to worry. There's a ship waiting at Ramsgate. They'll take us across the channel."

"You've given them the information they want." As loud as the motor was, I had to yell to make myself heard. "Why wouldn't they simply kill you?"

"After working five bloody years at the Committee of Imperial Defense I've amassed a great deal of information. It's all up here." He tapped his head. "I'm worth more alive."

"If that's the case, why did you sell document after document?"

"Appetizers, Miss Worthington, so they could see the kind of information that I had in my possession. Once that was done, I negotiated for more money. A lot more. I have an island in the Caribbean all picked out. I intend to live there the rest of my life." If he was sharing this much information, one thing was clear. Neither Lady Charlotte nor I would live to tell the tale. If we made it to that ship at Ramsgate, chances were we'd be tossed into the channel once we were far away from land.

"You think they'd let you live after you tell them everything you know?"

"I won't tell them everything. I'll hold something back."

Didn't he realize how ruthless these people were? They would torture him until they wrung every bit of information from him.

"You'd betray your own country."

He huffed. "What has England ever done for me?"

"As the son of an earl, you've lived all your life in the lap of luxury, Nicky," Lady Charlotte said.

"And every one of those days, Father told me how worthless I was. Marsh only cares about his heir. Second and third sons are only spares. And now that the heir has married and has a son of his own, I basically became surplus to requirements. I had to make my own mark in the world. And I have. I bloody well have."

"By betraying your country."

The motorboat hit something hard. Soon, it veered to the right.

"What was that?" Derwent asked.

"A bank, a rock, who knows?" Lady Charlotte answered.

"The Thames is bloody wide. Stay clear."

"I can't very well do so when I don't know where we are."

"You're supposed to be an excellent sailor."

"Even the most excellent sailor needs to be familiar with what lies below. I can't steer the boat if I don't know what's there."

Another bump, and I screamed.

"We're going to have to land the boat."

"We bloody well will not."

"Nicky. Something's wrong. If I don't stop to take a look, we might very well be dead in the water. It's nighttime. If another boat comes along, it might ram us, and we'd be toppled into the river. If memory serves me right, you don't know how to swim."

"Fine. How long will it take?"

"I'll try to be as quick as I can."

Somehow, we safely reached the shore. As soon as we did, Lady Charlotte pulled the motor out of the water. A blade was missing. "Well, that's that."

"Can't you fix it?" Nicky asked, clearly frustrated.

"No. I cannot. There's no fixing this. A new blade needs to be installed."

"Where are we?" I asked.

"I think that's Tilbury Fort," Lady Charlotte answered.

"That's not far from the coast," Derwent said. "There has to be a road somewhere close. Let's walk."

"You should leave us here. You'll make your way faster without us."

"I could shoot you instead. Dead women tell no tales."

"Dead women will get you hanged."

"They'd have to find me first."

I decided to take a different approach. "All of Scotland Yard, never mind local police and intelligence agents, will be looking for you. You'll need hostages if you want to survive."

He thought about it for a minute or so. "Um, you do have a point. Let's go."

"You'll need to untie me first."

He waved the gun at Lady Charlotte. "Just so you know, if you try anything, I'll shoot Miss Worthington."

"I won't," Lady Charlotte said. Ever so slowly, she untied me.

Once she was done, I pressed her hands. "Thank you."

"Quit your jabbering. We got to get going."

"Wait!" I said, stumbling to my feet.

"What now?" The man was reaching the end of his tether.

"My dress is soaking wet from lying at the bottom of the boat. If you want me to go on, I'll need to wrap that tarp around me." I pointed to the covering at the front of the boat.

"Oh, for heaven's sake." He breathed out a frustrated breath. "Very well," he said.

"You'll need to turn around," I said.

"Why?"

"I need to take off my gown. I'd just as soon not have you see me in my altogether."

"Not like I haven't seen a naked woman before."

"You haven't seen me!"

He huffed out a breath as he turned around. But before he could point the gun at Lady Charlotte, I drove a high round kick to his head.

He dropped like a stone.

"Oh, my word," Lady Charlotte exclaimed.

"Don't just stand there," I said. "Get the gun."

Once Charlotte did, I grabbed the rope he'd tied me up with and secured his hands and feet. "There."

"What do we do now?" Lady Charlotte asked.

I slid back into my dress. "Find a house. There's a light there in the distance." I pointed it out. "Hopefully they have a telephone."

It took us fifteen minutes to get there. To say the least, they were surprised to see two young ladies wandering round the countryside. They didn't have a telephone, but the constabulary did. Thankfully, it was just down the road.

After we introduced ourselves and I mentioned Chief Detective Inspector Robert Crawford Sinclair, we got their attention. Soon, Lady Charlotte was leading them back to where I'd dropped her cousin. I remained behind to wait for Robert to telephone. Twenty minutes later, he did.

"Where are you?"

"Milton Next Gravesend."

"How did you end up there?"

"Nicky Derwent kidnapped me and Lady Charlotte as well. I'll tell you the rest when you get here."

CHAPTER 33

EXPLANATIONS ARE MADE

*J*T WAS MORNING by the time we returned to Worthington House. Thankfully, Robert had sent word that I was with him and safe. As there was certain to be a fallout from the events of that night, I insisted Lady Charlotte stay with us, at least for the near future. She absolutely could not return home today. Maybe never.

The bedraggled aspect not only of myself but Lady Charlotte was bound to cause comment. But Carlton, consummate butler that he was, did not turn a hair and greeted us with his usual politeness. But then he always remained unflappable no matter the crisis. He informed us the family was enjoying breakfast.

Since we were in no shape to make an appearance in the dining room, we asked that some breakfast fare be brought to us in the drawing room. With all the excitement, I was starving. In the meantime, I would appreciate it if he informed Mother and Father about our arrival.

"Could you also let Mrs. Simpson know Lady Charlotte will be staying with us?" I asked.

"Of course, Miss," he said.

Having taken care of the important details, our bedraggled group made its way to the drawing room to await breakfast. But before it arrived, Mother and Father rushed in.

After one look at us, Mother exclaimed, "My goodness, Kitty."

"Mother, may I introduce Lady Charlotte, Marsh's niece. She will be staying with us for the near future."

Lady Charlotte curtsied. "I hope it's not an imposition, Mrs. Worthington."

"Of course not, dear. I've been eager to make your acquaintance. You're more than welcome to stay with us as long as you need." Mother could never be anything less than polite.

Father, on the other hand, couldn't contain his anger. "What the devil happened?" He barked out.

"Edward, please. Explanations can wait. Kitty and Lady Charlotte are safe. And, of course, dear Robert as well. That's all that matters for the moment."

Anything else he had to say was interrupted by footmen entering with trays of food, coffee, and tea.

But as soon as they withdrew, he made his point. "I will need a thorough explanation." He pinned his glare on Robert.

"And you will receive it, sir. But there are matters of national security that need to be dealt with before any of us can discuss last night's events."

We'd agreed on the way to London, we would not share any details until we'd been cleared as to what we could say. In the meantime, since we were all starving and in desperate need of sustenance, we addressed the food.

"Come Edward," Mother said, "let them enjoy their

breakfast in peace. I'll have Mrs. Simpson prepare a room for Lady Charlotte. The Lotus room, I think."

Lady Charlotte was caught with a bite in her mouth, but she had a definite question in her eyes.

"Mother has refurbished the bedchambers in the oriental style. They're all quite lovely."

Twenty minutes later, I could not eat another bite. All I wanted was a bath and my bed. But first I had to say goodbye to Robert.

"Heading home for a bath and a change of clothes, I imagine."

He nodded.

"And some sleep before you head back to Scotland Yard?" I asked hopefully.

All I received in return was an enigmatic smile.

"Come back when you can."

"I imagine it won't be until this evening."

"I'll be waiting." I placed my hand on his chest. "Please do try and get some rest."

A swift kiss and he was gone.

I returned to the drawing room to find Mrs. Simpson explaining things to Lady Charlotte. "Betsy will be assisting you until your lady's maid arrives."

"She's the best, Lady Charlotte," I said. "You can trust her to keep your confidences. She was my lady's maid before she turned receptionist for my detective agency."

"Thank you. You've all been so kind."

Arm in arm we climbed the stairs and proceeded to the Lotus Room where Betsy was waiting for her.

"You'll need to fetch your clothes from Marsh House. In the meantime, we can find something for you to wear. Lady Mellie is closest to you in size, and she has the same coloring. I'll ask her to lend you a gown or two."

"Oh, please I don't want to be that much trouble."

"No trouble at all. It gives her an excuse to buy new ones. Hollingsworth is very generous with her clothes allowance. Now, go get some rest."

"Thank you, dear Kitty. I don't know what would have happened to me if you weren't there."

"I could say the same. Go on."

Once she shut the door behind her, I headed toward my room. Along the way, I heard piano music. Had to be Lady Mellie. So, I wrote a note and asked Grace to deliver it to her maid. I was barely awake through my bath. So much so, Grace had to support me as I made my way to bed.

Hours later, I came slowly awake. The clock on the mantel told me it was half past six. I'd slept for nine hours.

Every muscle in my body objected as I tried to sit up. Ignoring the soreness, I prevailed. "Grace?"

She emerged from the sitting room. "Yes, Miss."

"Have we heard from Inspector Crawford Sinclair?"

"Not yet, Miss."

"What about dresses for Lady Charlotte?"

"Lady Mellie's maid delivered several to her room. Fresh undergarments as well. Oh, and dancing slippers."

I smiled. "I don't think Lady Charlotte will be attending a ball any time soon."

"They were the only ones we could find in her size. Mrs. Worthington wanted to send to a shop for new shoes. But Lady Mellie talked her out of it. Apparently, Lady Charlotte is very particular about her footwear. The mistress said you were only to join them if you felt up to it."

"There's no sense in postponing the inevitable, Grace. They'll have questions. Not that there is much I can say."

A few minutes before the cocktail hour, I knocked on Lady Charlotte's door. We might as well face the music together. She thrust open the door with a smile. The midnight blue gown suited her to a T.

"You look beautiful."

"It's a wonder what eight hours sleep, a hot bath, and fresh clothes can do."

"Ready to face the inquisition?"

"No time like the present."

We arrived at the drawing room to find an unusually large crowd. Family, of course, and all the ladies, including Monique. Plus Hollingsworth and Marlowe as well.

"Ladies Lily and Mellie immediately rushed us, kissed Lady Charlotte's cheek, hugged me. Lady Emma casually approached, shaking her head. "You get to have all the fun."

"I wouldn't exactly call it fun."

When she also embraced me, she had tears in her eyes. "No, it didn't sound like it was."

My face fell. "You know?"

"The papers got hold of the story. Lord Wallace and his House of Earthly Delights. I hear all the papers sold out within an hour."

"Just as well. Neither of us can discuss what happened."

A knock on the door later preceded Carlton's entrance. Robert had arrived, and, to my surprise, he was accompanied by Lord Salverton. Both were attired in formal evening wear. Neither appeared to have gotten much sleep.

Once he was introduced, Salverton made his role abundantly clear. "I'm only here to provide the official explanation, and then I'll be on my way."

"Nonsense," Mother said. "You'll stay for supper."

He offered her a courtly bow. "Thank you, ma'am."

"Whisky, or something else," Ned asked Salverton. He'd already handed a tumbler to Robert.

"Whisky will be fine."

While Salverton took up the narration, everyone accommodated themselves around the room.

"Yesterday, a confidential informant alerted us to shady

dealings about to take place at Lord Wallace's Woolwich estate. So we gathered a squad of experienced officers and headed there. While some remained outside, Marlowe and Sinclair made their way inside, as well as undercover officers adept at blending in."

"Where was Kitty during all this?" Father asked. Apparently, he'd had enough of waiting for an explanation.

"Er," Salverton said.

"I made my way there by myself." No way was I pointing the finger at Mister Clapham.

Father ground his teeth. "We'll talk about this later, young lady."

"Yes, sir."

"Due to unforeseen circumstances," Salverton continued, "the target made his getaway. Turned out he had a motorboat moored by the shore. He, er, had stolen it and kidnapped Lady Charlotte."

Gasps sounded all around the room.

"And Kitty?" Father asked.

"He kidnapped her as well."

"This master criminal," Father asked. "Does he have a name?"

"He does, but I'm not at liberty to reveal it at the moment. Although things will be made clearer over the coming weeks."

"I'm assuming they took the motorboat down the Thames?" Father asked.

"Yes."

"With Lady Charlotte at the tiller?" Father asked.

"Yes, sir."

"Maneuvering the Thames at night!" Hollingsworth exclaimed. "What a foolhardy thing to do."

"Well, seeing how he had a gun to our backs, Hollingsworth," I said, "we didn't have a choice."

Robert made a strangled sound.

"And where were you, sir," Father asked Robert, "when my daughter was in danger?"

"Don't blame Robert, Father. I was locked inside a room with my consent. I would have been safe, except . . ."

"Except," Father prompted.

"The house has tunnels that lead to the outside. The person who kidnapped me knew his way about. When we emerged, we were a quarter mile from the house in a field, close to the Thames. I believed I would find a way to escape, but after I saw Lady Charlotte, I knew I couldn't. He used each of us to threaten the other."

"Tell me he'll pay, Salverton," Father said.

"He will, sir. It's a hanging offense what he did. He murdered Lord Rosewood."

"Salverton!" I cautioned him as Monique cried out.

Mother, who'd sat near her, placed a comforting arm around Monique's shoulders.

"I beg your pardon, ma'am," Salverton said, addressing Monique. "It's been a rather long day."

"Couple of days," I corrected. "You need to go home and rest. You too, Robert. No need to stay for supper."

"Are you sure?" Robert asked.

"Both of you are ready to drop on your feet. You've done your duty. Go home. We'll talk in the morning."

CHAPTER 34

ALL'S WELL THAT ENDS WELL

*M*ATTERS AT SCOTLAND YARD demanded Robert's full attention, so we did not talk the next day. But Father and I did. He threatened to shut down the agency if I ever did such a foolhardy thing again. I believed him. After all he held the purse strings. But even more important, he was right. My recklessness had almost cost me my life.

For the following week, the House of Earthly Delights scandal was front page news. It was all anyone could talk about. As a consequence, Lord Rosewood's murder was relegated to the second page. Nicky Derwent officially confessed to the crime. After a swift trial, he was sentenced to solitary confinement for the rest of his life. He should have ended up at the gallows.

More than likely, he was given the lighter sentence in exchange for information about the foreign spy network. I had nothing to base that on other than my intuition. Robert hadn't mentioned it, and neither had Salverton.

His treasonous acts didn't make the news. Made sense. The government couldn't afford for the public to know.

For national security reasons, Lord Marsh's perfidy was just as quietly dealt with. Within days of his son's sentencing, he announced he was seriously ill and would retire to Marsh Castle. He would never be Lord High Chancellor, but he'd get to keep his title and fortune. Not that it would do him much good. When word got around about what he'd done, he became persona non grata among his peers. No one would attend future suppers nor issue invitations. He was bound to lead a lonely existence until his death.

Lady Charlotte remained with us. Something she was more than happy to do as she wanted nothing more to do with her uncle or the Marsh name. To her surprise, she discovered she'd inherited a quite sizable fortune from her father who'd invested in business matters in the Far East. As soon as she became aware of that fact, she asked Ned to arrange for a solicitor to transfer the management of her estate to Worthington & Son.

"And to think Marsh complained about the measly allowance he handed me every month," she huffed when she found out. "I could just spit nails."

"Well, the good news is you're a wealthy heiress," I said. "You can do whatever your heart desires."

Her gaze took on a faraway look. "There's only one thing I really want. To see the world. In a ship, if it can be arranged."

"Ummm," was my only answer. I could see where this was headed.

The day after she learned about her wealth, Hollingsworth came to supper. She waited until after the meal to approach him.

"May I have a word with you, Lord Hollingsworth?"

"Of course," he replied. Never let it be said that he was anything less than polite.

She led him to an area of the drawing room where they could hold a private conversation. I had no shame, so I took a stroll to a space close enough to overhear without appearing intrusive and claimed a spot on a settee.

"What are you doing?" Robert asked approaching me.

"Shhh, I'm trying to listen in on Lady Charlotte and Hollingsworth's conversation. Sit down before they see you."

He gazed in their direction. "Unless you have the hearing of a bat, I doubt you can."

I frowned at him. "Especially if you keep talking. Now sit down and hush."

Sporting a wicked smile, he joined me in the settee. "I thought we could discuss the sketches of the china patterns you sent me."

I'd sketched out a few ideas and sent them to him. "Now?"

"No time like the present."

I ground my teeth.

But there was no stopping him. "The bloodied fish in the swan's beak was an interesting choice. It might put our guests off their feed, though. They might be inclined never to accept another supper invitation from us."

I turned my attention fully to him. "Is that so?"

"And then there's the one with a gentleman being chased by yet another swan. A masterful rendition. Although to be true to the legend, he should be depicted sans trousers."

I laughed. "It was a joke, Robert."

He laughed right back. "Really? You could have fooled me."

"I've never fooled you, not that I haven't tried."

For a while, we just gazed at each other, supremely content to be in each other's company. But then, Robert nodded toward Hollingsworth and Lady Charlotte. "What are they discussing?"

"Lady Charlotte wants to sail on Hollingsworth's ship."

"Absolutely not," Hollingsworth exclaimed loud enough for me to hear.

"Well, there's your answer," Robert said.

I scoffed. "As if Lady Charlotte would give up that easily."

But at least for the moment their conversation was finished. Hollingsworth and Lady Charlotte sailed past us to rejoin the other guests. Only time would tell if she'd be able to convince him.

The Ladies of Distinction Detective Agency continued to thrive. As my involvement in the House of Earthly Delights scandal never came to light, it had no effect on our caseload. We were as busy as ever.

Ned met with Lady Emma and me. The law being what it was, we couldn't own the agency by ourselves. So the three of us formed a partnership. The compromise seemed acceptable to Lady Emma. Now that she was a named principal, she was happy enough. We determined not to make any changes for the moment. In the spring we would revisit both a move to larger quarters and hiring additional staff, if indeed there was a need for either at that time.

The charges against Maurice Gautier were officially dropped. But only after Robert and Scotland Yard pressured the Crown Prosecution Service. The Service argued a conspiracy had existed between Maurice Gautier and Nicky Derwent. As there was no proof they'd even met, and there was plenty that Derwent had obtained the information from August Baudet, they finally relented.

Monique remained with us while justice dealt with Lord Rosewood's murderer. Needless to say, she was not happy about the life sentence. She felt he should have been consigned to the gallows. But when I explained there were matters of national importance at play, she resigned herself to the outcome.

On a happier note, the new Lord Rosewood reached out to her. He wished to visit before he departed for Cornwall with Lord Heathcote, his new guardian. He would spend the rest of the summer there before he returned to Eton in the fall.

For an hour, they enjoyed a private conversation in which he expressed his desire to remain in touch. He was overjoyed when Monique told him she was expecting a baby. Apparently, he'd always wished for a sibling. And now, he had his wish. By the time they parted, Monique felt she'd been truly accepted by the Rosewood family. At least the one who mattered.

"How is his ankle?" I asked. After the reading of the will, Monique had asked me about the cause of the young Lord Rosewood's injury. So she was conversant with it.

"Much better. He's barely limping now."

"That's good to hear. Did he explain how it happened?" After my conversation with Robert, he'd paid a visit to Rosewood House in his own persona. But he hadn't been able to to get to the truth.

"He confessed the fall down the stairs had been his fault. He was so busy reading a book, he missed a step."

That was a relief. "Why didn't he say so before?"

"He was too embarrassed. You know what young men of that age are like."

"I do." My brother Richard came to mind. As a child, he was always searching for buried treasure in the back garden, once going so far as to dig up Mother's favorite blooms. An honest mistake for he hadn't recognized what they were. He apologized profusely. But he'd been so embarrassed the tips of his ears had grown quite red.

"William asked me to think of him as a son," she said

laughing. "But I can't do that, I'm only four years older than him."

"Then think of him as a friend."

"Yes. A dear friend."

A week later, Maurice was well enough to be released from the hospital. So she arranged a move back to the house Rosewood had purchased for her. Once Maurice was fit enough to travel, they would relocate to Paris where she planned to give birth and raise her child in the city she and Rosewood had fallen in love.

"We'll miss you," I said when she told me.

"As I will miss you, but this is something I must do. Not only for Maury's sake, but my own. I have to . . . find my life again."

"It will be different."

"Yes." She curled a hand around her middle. "A baby will be a big change. But he, or she, will grow up knowing it's dearly loved."

"You have such a gift, Monique. Will you sing again?"

She bit back a smile. "About that."

CHAPTER 35

ONE LAST SONG

 $\mathcal{M}$ ONIQUE HAD ARRANGED A SURPRISE for us. A concert to be held at Gennaro's. A final performance if you will before she dedicated her life to raising her child.

Her reason for the concert was twofold. For one, she felt she owed Gennaro. He'd hired a jazz band with a singer, and she'd been missing for the last month. Gennaro had assured her he didn't hold her responsible. But he hadn't said no when she'd made the offer.

The other reason was to thank the Worthington family and Robert. Without our help, she would have never made it through. So she wished to dedicate this special performance to us.

Gennaro was not slow to take advantage of it. The businessman in him saw the value of one last performance by the talented Monique Gautier. He sold tickets to the event.

Once they went on sale, the event sold out within hours.

Predictably, those who hadn't managed to buy one were soon clamoring for one more concert. But Gennaro put paid to that notion. Miss Gautier would sing at one performance and no more.

On the night of the concert, Robert and I, along with our family and friends, were welcomed as her special guests. As far as I knew Mother and Father had never visited a jazz club. But even they were there. The club's security staff had been increased for the night. In case somebody caused a scene, they would be removed immediately and taken to the nearest constabulary.

Our tickets had been provided for free. Robert, however, paid for his. As he was a Scotland Yard Chief Detective Inspector, anything gratis could be considered a bribe. The rest of our group were given no choice. Gennaro himself told us he would issue no check, nor would he accept payment from any of us.

The concert did not last long, maybe an hour. But that hour was magical. As Monique sang one song after another, her talent was in full display. Some of her choices were lively; others were sad. And then there was the last one.

A visibly emotional Monique stood at the microphone. "There are some people I wish to acknowledge. First, the members of the Rhythm Kings Jazz Band. They gave a seventeen-year-old girl from the bayou of New Orleans a rare gift —the opportunity to shine. I'll be forever grateful." She pointed back to them and applauded. The crowd enthusiastically joined her.

"I also want to thank my brother, Maurice. When he heard his skinny little sister warbling in the kitchen, he encouraged her to sing. First in church and then in a local club close to home. Thanks to him, I've traveled to New York, Chicago, Paris, and now London. You will be forever close to my heart, dear brother." She pointed to him. "Stand up, Maury."

As Maurice stood on wobbly legs, a smattering of applause greeted him. Although he was on the mend, it was clear he was still healing. But he considered himself fortunate. He was alive and breathing.

She took a deep breath and announced, "This will be my last song."

Predictably, the crowd objected. But once she gestured for silence, they quieted.

"As such, I want to dedicate it to two dear friends who fought to gain justice for my brother and protected me, Miss Catherine Worthington and Chief Detective Inspector Robert Crawford Sinclair. If you don't know, they're getting married in the fall. Thank you from the bottom of my heart. I'll never forget you. Please take a bow."

"Well, this is awkward," I said coming to my feet along with Robert.

"Just smile and wave to the crowd," he said.

To my surprise, there was a wild applause, almost as much as Monique had received.

The crowd quieted as we retook our seats. And then the band struck up a song I adored.

It had to be you. It had to be you.
I wandered around and finally found the somebody who
Could make me be true. Could make me be blue.
I even was glad just to be sad thinking of you.

When Simone blew us a kiss, I searched for Robert's hand and found it.

Some others I've seen have tried to be mean.
Have tried to be cross. Tried to be boss.

But they wouldn't do.
For nobody else gave me that thrill.
With all your faults, I love you still.
It had to be you. Wonderful You. It had to be You.

As the last note died down, everyone jumped to their feet and applause rained down on Monique. But even as she acknowledged the accolade, a tinge of sadness was clearly visible on her face. The man she'd loved was gone.

THE CONCERT HAD ENDED at ten which meant the evening was still young. Other than Mother and Father who eagerly sought their beds, no one wished to retire for the night. So, we gathered at Worthington House for drinks and refreshments.

"What will happen to Miss Gautier?" Lady Delphine asked. She wasn't familiar with Monique's plans.

"She inherited Rosewood's apartment in Paris. So she plans to return there to bear her child."

"And Maurice?"

"He will travel to Paris with her. I imagine he'll remain there. They don't have any family left in New Orleans."

"Even with her brother for company, she'll be so alone in Paris," Lady Lily said. "I couldn't imagine not having my family around me."

"I, for one, plan to keep in touch. You can write her as well. I'm sure she'll love to hear from you. And Lady Mellie as well."

"I was planning to do so," Lady Mellie said. "Maybe even visit next spring after her baby is born."

"I'm sure she'd love that," I said.

"Paris can be a very expensive city," Lady Delphine said.

She didn't know about Monique's inheritance. While we carried out the investigation, we'd kept that information to ourselves. But now there was no longer a need to do so.

"Oh, she won't need to worry about money, Lady Delphine. Rosewood bequeathed her a very comfortable amount. She asked Worthington & Son to manage it for her. A Parisian associate of the firm will deal with her monthly expenses."

"Speaking about investments, Worthington," Marlowe directed the comment toward Ned, "I've been rethinking my investment strategies. Do you have any recommendations?"

"Invest in property, both here and in the United States. People will always need land to build on."

"What about the American stock market?" Marlowe asked. "Everyone's buying shares, it seems."

Ned shook his head. "Father and I don't see that as a solid investment. Too many people are buying on margins, meaning they're borrowing money to buy shares. That drives up their cost. With no solid capitalization to uphold that value, it could spell disaster."

"Some people see it as a way to quick wealth."

"A get-rich-quick scheme rarely works. We try to educate our clients, but some won't listen. If our vision doesn't match theirs, we part ways. We won't compromise our principles."

"Goodness," I said. "That's much too serious a discussion on such a glorious night. Let's go have some fun."

"Where?" Lady Charlotte asked.

"Follow me, and you'll find out." I led them to the ball-room where the staff had set up everything the way I requested.

Lady Mellie was the first to spot it. "Ooh, a gramophone and recordings. Wherever did you get them?"

"A music shop on Denmark Street opened up recently. They're selling them."

She rushed to pick up the recordings. As she lovingly handled them, she called out the song titles—*Livery Stable Blues, Tea for Two, Charleston, Five Feet Two, Eyes of Blue.* She turned back toward us. "I wonder if there's sheet music for all of these."

"I'm sure there is," I said approaching her. "Now, what should we play first?"

"Charleston, of course."

After the tune began playing, I turned back to Robert. "Shall we?"

He shook his head but wasn't slow to take me up on my invitation. Soon, everyone was kicking up their heels, tossing their arms in the air, and laughing gayly.

But after a while, they all drifted away—some to the drawing room, others to bed. Ned and Lady Lily more than likely headed to another room where they could enjoy a bit of privacy. Soon, the only ones left were Robert and me.

I approached the gramophone and dropped a new recording into it—*Tea for Two.* When the song started playing, Robert spun me around and started dancing with me.

Picture me upon your knee
Just tea for two and two for tea
Just me for you and you for me alone.
Nobody near us to see us or to hear us
No friends or relations on weekend vacations
We won't have it known, dear
That we own a telephone, dear.

"No telephone calls might pose a problem for Scotland Yard, dear," Robert said twirling me.

"Maybe they can employ smoke signals."

Day will break and I'll awake

And start to bake a sugar cake
For you to take for all the boys to see.

"Just so you know," I said. "I can't bake."
He grinned. "You have other talents."

We will raise a family
A boy for you and a girl for me
Oh, can't you see how happy we would be?

As we stopped dancing, he grew dead serious. "Will we be happy, darling?"

"Inspector," I said wrapping my arms around him, "I guarantee it."

And then he kissed me, proving my point.

∽

DID you enjoy **Murder at the Jazz Club**? Read on to discover Kitty Worthington's next adventure.

A Murder at Brighton

With her wedding day rapidly approaching, all Kitty Worthington wants is a fun seaside holiday with her loved ones. But some are at outs with each other, the weather's not promising, and someone gets murdered. Again.

Brighton 1924. The pleasant vacation **Kitty Worthington** envisioned is not going well. Disagreements and altercations between those dear to her all too soon scuttle her plans. Determined to enjoy some fun in the sun, she heads to the shore with her fiancé, **Chief Detective Inspector Crawford Sinclair**. But before they can dip their toes in the surf, they stumble across the body of a wealthy socialite. In their beach hut, of all places.

As bad luck would have it, Kitty's intended is soon assigned the case. After all, he's not only present, but experienced at solving murders of the elite. Eager to salvage what's left of her holiday, Kitty offers to help. To her surprise, so do her family and friends.

But finding the murderer won't be easy. The woman was roundly disliked. Did the milquetoast husband kill her? Or was it the much put upon stepdaughter? And what about the shady stepson in debt up to his ears?

With a raging storm bearing down on them, there's no time to lose. Witnesses and suspects are all jumping ship. And if that weren't enough, the Worthingtons' beloved basset hound soon goes missing along with the murder victim's pooch. Is it a ploy of the murderer or an unfortunate coincidence? Whatever the reason, they must discover the killer before all is lost.

A Murder at Brighton, Book 8 in The Kitty Worthington Mysteries. This 1920s historical cozy mystery set at a glamorous Brighton seaside resort is sure to please lovers of Agatha Christie and Downton Abbey alike.

~

HAVE you read the first Kitty Worthington Mystery? **Murder on the Golden Arrow**, Book 1 in the Kitty Worthington Mysteries, is available on Amazon and Kindle Unlimited

What's a bright young woman to do when her brother becomes the main suspect in a murder? Why, solve the case of course.

England. 1923. After a year away at finishing school where she learned etiquette, deportment, and the difference between a salad fork and a fish one, Kitty Worthington is eager to return home. But minutes after she and her brother Ned board the Golden Arrow, the unthinkable happens. A woman with a mysterious connection to her brother is poisoned, and the murderer can only be someone aboard the train.

When Scotland Yard hones in on Ned as the main suspect, Kitty sets out to investigate. Not an easy thing to do while juggling the demands of her debut season and a mother intent on finding a suitable, aristocratic husband for her.

With the aid of her maid, two noble beaus, and a flatulent basset hound named Sir Winston, Kitty treads a fearless path through the glamorous world of high society and London's dark underbelly to find the murderer. For if she fails, the insufferable Inspector Crawford will most surely hang a noose around her brother's neck.

Murder on the Golden Arrow, Book 1 in The Kitty Worthington Mysteries. A historical cozy mystery filled with dodgy suspects, a dastardly villain, and an intrepid heroine sure to win your heart. Available on Amazon and Kindle Unlimited

CAST OF CHARACTERS

Kitty Worthington - Our sleuth

The Worthington Family
    Mildred Worthington - Kitty's mother
    Edward Worthington - Kitty's father
    Ned Worthington - Kitty's oldest brother
    Richard Worthington - Kitty's next oldest brother, currently in Egypt

The Worthington Household
    Grace Flanagan - Kitty's maid
    Carlton - the family butler
    Mrs. Simpson - the family housekeeper
    Neville - the family chauffeur and Betsy's beau
    Mrs. Cutler - Cook and Betsy's aunt
    James - Footman
    Sir Winston - Family's beloved basset hound

The Ladies of Distinction Detective Agency

Lady Emma Carlyle - Kitty's friend and partner in the Ladies of Distinction Detective Agency

Lady Aurelia Holmes - Assistant lady detective

Betsy Robson - Receptionist and assistant at the Ladies of Distinction Detective Agency, formerly Kitty's personal maid

Owen Clapham - former Scotland Yard detective inspector, aids with investigations

The Wynchcombe Family and Household

His Grace the Duke of Wynchcombe, Sebastian Dalrymple - married to Margaret, Kitty's sister

Her Grace the Duchess of Wynchcombe, Margaret Dalrymple - Kitty's older sister, now married to the Duke of Wynchcombe

Lady Lily Dalrymple - Sebastian's sister, enjoying her debut season

Temple - the Duke of Wynchcombe's London butler

The Rosewood Family

Lord Rosewood - a marquis

Lord Stephen - Lord Rosewood's younger brother

Lord William - Lord Rosewood's son

Lord Heathcote - Lord Rosewood's maternal uncle

The Rhythm Kings Jazz Band and Staff

Samuel 'King' Tibideaux - the band leader - Cornet

Isidore 'Izzy' Bonom - Drums

Jubal Johnson - Bass

Baptiste Dupin - Clarinet

Paul Jackson - Trombone

Thibaut Turner - Guitar

Augustine 'August' Baudet - Piano

Monique Gautier - Singer

Maurice Gautier - Security Guard and Monique's brother

The Marsh Family and Household
Lord Marsh - an earl
Lady Charlotte - Lord Marsh's niece
Nicholas Derwent - Lord Marsh's third son

Other Notable Characters
Chief Detective Inspector Robert Crawford Sinclair from Scotland Yard and Kitty's fiancé
Lord Hollingsworth - A marquis, explorer and adventurer and Robert Crawford Sinclair's friend
Lady Melissande - Lord Hollingsworth's sister and a debutante
Lord Marlowe - An earl - attracted to Lady Emma
Lord Salverton - A marquis- friend of Lord Hollingsworth
Lady Delphine – Kitty's friend - plans to open a modiste shop
Claudine - Monique Gautier's lady's maid

Made in United States
Troutdale, OR
01/25/2024

17130394R00159